Lisa Stringfellow

A Comb of Wishes

Quill Tree Books
An Imprint of HarperCollinsPublishers

Quill Tree Books is an imprint of HarperCollins Publishers.
A Comb of Wishes
Text copyright © 2022 by Lisa Stringfellow
All rights reserved. Printed in the United States of America.
No part of this book may be used or reproduced in any manner
whatsoever without written permission except in the case of
brief quotations embodied in critical articles and reviews. For
information address HarperCollins Children's Books, a division of
HarperCollins Publishers, 195 Broadway, New York, NY 10007.
www.harpercollinschildrens.com

Library of Congress Cataloging-in-Publication Data
Names: Stringfellow, Lisa, 1970- author.
Title: A comb of wishes / Lisa Stringfellow.
Description: First edition. | New York : Quill Tree Books, an
    imprint of HarperCollins Publishers, [2022] | Audience: Ages
    8-12. | Audience: Grades 4-6. | Summary: Twelve-year-old
    Kela is still mourning her mother when she finds a mermaid's
    comb while she and her friend are looking for sea glass on
    her Caribbean island; such combs have magic in them, and
    touching it opens a connection to the mermaid Ophidia who
    can grant her wish, to bring her mother back to life—but all
    wishes have consequences, and magic demands a price which
    may prove to be more painful than the loss of her mother.
Identifiers: LCCN 2021030796 | ISBN 9780063043435 (hardcover)
Subjects: LCSH: Mermaids—Juvenile fiction. | Magic—Juvenile
    fiction. | Wishes—Juvenile fiction. | Sea glass—Juvenile
    fiction. | Grief—Juvenile fiction. | Mothers and daughters—
    Juvenile fiction. | Friendship—Juvenile fiction. | Caribbean
    Area—Juvenile fiction. | CYAC: Mermaids—Fiction. |
    Magic—Fiction. | Wishes—Fiction. | Sea glass—Fiction.
    | Grief—Fiction. | Mothers and daughters—Fiction. |
    Friendship—Fiction. | Caribbean Area—Fiction.
Classification: LCC PZ7.1.S7956 Co 2022 | DDC 813.6 [Fic]—dc23
LC record available at https://lccn.loc.gov/2021030796

Typography by David Curtis
21 22 23 24 25   PC/LSCH   10 9 8 7 6 5 4 3 2 1
❖
First Edition

To my father and grandparents,
who live in these pages

To M, B, and A,
so you remember to dream

Contents

CHAPTER 1
Crick, Crack

I say Crick, you say Crack.
Crick.
Crack.
This is a story.

Down past the islands lit by the sun, beyond twilight swells of dusky sea, through midnight veils of the crushing abyss, another world hides under the waves. The other side of the mirror, as it is known.

Through these depths swam a sea woman. The full moon rose and spilled its milk into the water, and light glimmered over dark brown skin. Her scales flashed green and gold.

Foreboding drifted on the tide and urged her on.

When she reached the cavern, the quiet struck her first. No gentle trill greeted her as it usually did. In her hiding place only a broken tumble of rocks and stones remained.

Hope dissolved as she groped through the cavern, trembling. Her tail fin thrashed as she plunged her arms into every corner. But the silence told her that the box was gone.

Her pupils narrowed to dangerous slits.

The sea woman rode the cold current into the briny deep. She would reclaim the box—and what was inside. She must.

Time and tides would decide.

Crick.

Crack.

The story is put on you.

CHAPTER 2

Sinking Sand

The note waited on the kitchen table. Kela didn't even have to pick it up or read Pop's blocky print to know what it said.

Her fingers hesitated over the paper. She and Pop hadn't gone diving or done anything normal together in months. She missed the salty mist on her face and the trampolining waves.

Kela lifted the note and balled it in her fist.

She took a deep breath, then shut the door of the empty house.

The gravel crunched under Kela's feet as she crossed the street into a dense patch of trees. A foot-worn path wound its way between towering cabbage palms and sandbox trees. The gully sloped and she stepped around the snaking roots of a bearded fig. Leaves rustled overhead—a monkey skittered across a bough.

With the push of a branch, the forest ended. Kela looked out at the waves lapping the shore. The beach. The one place that felt like home.

She walked along the water's edge, her canvas bag hanging lightly from her shoulder.

When Kela was five, she had found the first piece of sea glass, blue like a cloudless sky. "You found a mermaid's tear!" Mum had said. "Let's try to find a whole rainbow." They had found every color but orange, the rarest. Now Kela stayed up at night thinking about that last piece. Mum's piece.

Kela peeked into her bag at what she had collected that week. Several pieces of sea glass, sharp edges worn away by water and sand. The colors rippled like the surf. Translucent green, white, and a piece that glowed golden amber.

Her mother had taught her to make jewelry from these gems of the sea. When something caught her eye, she'd try to imagine how a person could wear it. A charm hanging from a crocheted necklace. Wrapped in wire to make an anklet. She never knew exactly what she was going to make until she got started. In these broken bits of glass, trash to some, Kela saw possibilities, the broken made beautiful.

She took out a piece and held it to the sky. Green brightness spilled softly into her hand. She remembered the old island folktale about sea glass. Could sadness really make something so beautiful?

"Kela?"

Kela turned toward the voice and her face fell. Her friend Lissy stepped out from the trees and walked to her.

"How'd you know I'd be here?" Kela asked in a low voice.

"Where else would you be?" Lissy replied. "But ever since . . ." She paused, her eyes searching the water as if the right words would jump out like flying fish. "It just seems like you always come without me now."

Kela dropped the sea glass she was holding back into her bag. Lissy was right. Three months ago, they would have been on this beach together.

"Did I do something wrong?" Lissy's brown eyes stared fixedly at Kela.

"No," Kela said. She shifted her feet.

"I know things are hard," Lissy said softly. "I hear Gran talking with your dad." She looked down. "Whatever you're feeling—we don't have to talk about it. But we can if you want."

Kela remembered the fun she and Lissy once had together. Exploring the beach. Watching the sanderlings scoot along the shore. She'd pushed Lissy's friendship away, and like diving with Pop, she'd missed that too.

"All right," Kela said.

Lissy squeezed Kela's hand and pulled a bag out of her own pocket.

"Did you find any sea glass yet?"

"Some," Kela said with a slight smile. "But there's not much here."

"Let's head up the beach, then," Lissy said.

The shore snaked before them and the girls followed the tide line, raking the sand with their feet as they looked for treasure.

A heart-shaped pebble was the first to disappear into Kela's canvas bag. Small pieces of driftwood, sea beans, and a couple of pieces of sea glass went into the salty folds. She didn't collect shells.

Pop had explained how important shells were when she was little. They prevented beach erosion, provided homes and hiding places for animals, and were even food for creatures that lived in the sand. "If you want to keep St. Rita beautiful," he had said, "leave them where you find them."

But sea glass? That was just the sea returning what people had thrown away.

"The jewelry you left with Gran is some of your best," Lissy said. "Are you still planning to apply to the Creative Arts Program?"

"I don't know," Kela said quietly. When she first learned of the program for gifted young Caribbean artists, it had seemed perfect: twelve weeks of inspiring classes full of happy, carefree kids. Like the kind she used to be. She changed the subject.

"What have you been up to?" Kela asked. This was the most she and Lissy had talked in weeks.

"Oh, the usual," Lissy said. "Helping Gran in the shop. Business is picking up now that it's tourist season. She lets me help on the register."

Lissy's gran, Miss Inniss sold everything from sunglasses to homemade coconut sweet bread. And Kela's jewelry.

"That makes sense. You're good with math."

"Keep me company tomorrow," Lissy said. "Promise!" She stuck out her pinkie finger almost like she wanted to challenge Kela's teacup manners.

Kela wanted to laugh, but her stomach rolled. In her twelve years, she had never broken a pinkie promise with Lissy.

She hooked her pinkie with Lissy's.

"I promise."

Farther down the beach, they came to a tall wooden fence that extended from the hill to the water's edge. A large sign read "CORAL GARDENS CAVE—No Trespassing."

They were at the border of one of St. Rita's most beautiful nature parks. Hidden beneath the ground were sea-facing caves, natural rock pools, and a coral floor.

But it was also off-limits. Not only was access monitored with security cameras, it was dangerous to enter from this side of the park. Pop had often warned her that a wrong step on the slippery rocks could mean a nasty gash or, even worse, a steep fall and a broken neck.

"Maybe we'll have better luck tomorrow," Lissy said, kicking the sand and turning back the way they had come.

"Yeah," Kela said. She turned too, then stopped.

A faint warbling hum like the singing of tree frogs floated on the breeze. She scanned the thick green hillside, but she wasn't sure where it was coming from. What was it? Lissy walked ahead and didn't seem to notice.

"Do you hear that?" Kela asked.

"Hear what?"

"That sound. I think it's coming from up the hill."

Lissy turned. "I don't hear anything."

Part of Kela knew she should let it go, but the sound called to her. She remembered the stories of magic that Mum had read to her. Lissy couldn't hear it. Maybe it was just for Kela.

"I want to see where it's coming from," Kela said.

Lissy blinked. "You mean, climb up there?" She tilted her head in the direction of the slope.

"Just for a minute." Kela scrambled up the bank. "Watch your step."

"Kela!" Lissy stumbled behind her. "We're not supposed to go up there."

Kela clambered up the steep hill, over tree roots and rocks. Her foot slipped, but she grabbed a palm frond to steady herself.

The warbling hum trilled again, louder and more insistent. She cocked her head to pinpoint the sound. At the top of the hill, the ground leveled. A tree had fallen on a fence, splintering the wooden slats and creating an opening into the nature park.

"Wait!" Lissy huffed behind her. "Why are you doing this?"

Lissy was right. Pop would be furious if he knew she was here. And if the park's security found them, they'd be in even more trouble.

Kela turned to her friend. "I have to look."

She wished she could explain, but the feeling refused to be wrapped up in words. It was as if the strange humming sound had flowed over and around the pieces of Kela's broken heart—and her heart wanted more. I hear you. I'm coming!

Kela climbed carefully over the tree and onto the other side of the fence. Lissy hesitated, then followed in silent acceptance.

A short distance away, Kela stopped. The hum pulsed loud in her ears.

The rocky ground had crumbled to form a sinkhole. Faint light glowed from below and Kela could see rough outcrops of rock that angled down.

"What's down there?" she whispered, crouching low to peer into the pit.

Lissy shook her head. "You can't . . . What if you get hurt?"

"I'll be careful," Kela said, turning backward and inching her way down. Step by slow step, she probed for solid footing and lowered her body into the void.

She didn't realize she had been holding her breath until her feet touched bottom. She turned and squinted into the expanse of the cave.

An angular shape crouched in the sand a few feet ahead. Not rocks. Perhaps trash that had washed in from the ocean. It rested curiously out of place.

"Kela! Are you all right?" Lissy called. Her voice echoed off the cave walls.

"I'm fine," Kela replied, waving at her friend, who was lying flat on the ground at the top of the hole. "Give me a minute."

As she focused on the dim shape, the air bit with unnatural cold. Her skin pricked as she stepped gingerly across the sharp rocks. She extended her hand, undecided, then pulled the object from the coarse grit.

The hum stopped.

It was a box. A little bigger than the size of her hand and completely battered, nothing but barnacles and sea-worn wood. Its hinges oozed a rusty red. A tiny keyhole stared from its center.

Nothing betrayed its contents as she turned it over in her hands.

Kela looked around. When diving, there were rules about what you could take depending on where you were. But she wasn't diving now. Still, this was a protected nature park, which meant the box was protected too.

A public nature park belonged to the people. She was St. Ritan. What's here belongs to me too, at least in part, she reasoned.

Kela felt like she was in one of Mum's folktales. The box breathed a strangeness she couldn't shake. Small and crumbling, it seemed harmless. Her ears pounded with indecision.

Everything else had been taken from her. Yet here was something as lost and alone as she was. And it had called to her—had wanted her to find it.

"Kela!" Lissy yelled again.

"I'm coming!"

Kela's fingers tightened around the box, and she shoved it into her bag.

CHAPTER 3

Storm and Fury

Crick.

Crack.

This is a story.

Chasing the beats of her heart, the sea woman's chest heaved as she swam.

"Calm yourself, Ophidia."

Dusky waters caressed her face, reminding her that she was not alone. Even in the blackest trench, her mother's ancient voice echoed.

"You are not new-spawned," the sea whispered. "Use me to find what you need."

Water flowed through the slits on her neck as Ophidia closed her eyes and slowed her breathing.

She opened her mind to the currents. Memories seeped into her body.

The cavern waited as she had left it. Then, the seabed shook with unexpected force. Sand poured over coral banks like waterfalls, and vibrations buckled the ocean floor.

The cleft where she had so carefully hidden her box crumbled. Currents rushed and pulled it to the ocean floor. Tossed on the tides, it tumbled and pitched, until waves washed it into a place between land and sea, a coral cave. There it slumped, exposed and unprotected in the warm pools of salt and sand.

A membrane flicked across Ophidia's unblinking eyes. The memory continued.

Tides rose and fell, light glowed and died—and still the box waited for her.

Then, two hazy forms appeared.

Ophidia's lips pulled back in a guttural hiss. Humans. The dry rasp of their breathing grated in her ears. The sea woman bared her chiseled teeth. Powerless to change a memory, she watched.

One of the forms descended through a jagged hole into the cavern and found the age-blackened box. The human studied it, with no inkling of what it sheltered, then slipped it into a sack.

The image faded, and Ophidia's mind shifted back to the ruined cavern. Her fear of death bled out by its dark twin. Anger.

She unfurled her rage. Like poison, it oozed. Waves swelled and churned, and the sky mirrored the waters. Rain and wind ripped the sky and exploded in a storm of emotion.

"Be still . . ." The sea's words pierced her fury. "What is lost will return." The current cooled the heat of her cheeks and settled the inky coils of her hair.

Relenting, Ophidia resolved to trust the sea. And magic.

She had once ignored the wisdom of the sea and had paid a terrible price. Her tail twitched. The memory rankled, and she pushed it away.

When a human opened her box and touched what was inside, she would know. Magic required that she make a bargain. A wish, in exchange for what she had taken long ago.

Her box might easily return, and the one who had taken it might feel blessed. But blessings did not always happen. A smile touched Ophidia's lips. In some bargains, only she received what she wanted.

If she failed? In moonlight and foam, death would take her. Her tail flicked, a silent vow she would not allow that to happen.

Crick.
Crack.
The story is put on you.

CHAPTER 4
Legends and Lore

A sharp crack made Kela turn quickly.

"What was that?" Lissy yelled.

Kela didn't know. The atmosphere had changed. The air weighed heavy and damp on her skin, and her eyes squinted in the fading light. A rumbling drone rose high on the wind. The crack rang out again and Kela turned to see water surging in. In an instant, she knew. The sound was waves banking off the cave.

The tide was coming in. Fast.

Kela scrambled back to the sinkhole.

"The tide's rising!" she shouted to Lissy.

"Hurry up!" Her friend thrust out her hand.

Kela grabbed Lissy's outstretched hand, but her

damp palm slipped and she fell back, scraping her knee against the rocks. The bag slid off her shoulder. She reached to catch it, but her fingers grasped empty air. The crack rang out again as the bag bounced hard off the rocks and careened back to the cave floor.

Blood trickled down Kela's shaking leg. The wind howled and spit salty spray.

"Leave it!" Lissy yelled into the echoing hole.

Kela shook her head. She had come this far. It had called her. There was no way she was leaving without the box. She wiped her hand on her shorts and gripped the wall tight before lowering her body back down the face of the rock. When her feet touched the bottom, she grabbed the bag and slung it across her chest before she climbed again. At the top of the sinkhole, Lissy grabbed Kela's hand with both of hers and pulled Kela free.

The sky churned gray and black, and sand pelted their skin like needles. Kela and Lissy stumbled across the fence and slid back down the hill. With the damp bag thumping against Kela's side, they ran across the beach toward town.

Back at Kela's house, they heard the shrill *brrrng, brrrng* of the phone from the kitchen.

"Where have you been?" Pop asked when Kela picked up. "Didn't you see my note? I thought you'd be at the shop by now." His voice was sharp, but there was more worry in it than anger.

"At the beach," Kela said, trying to catch her breath. "We were looking for sea glass."

"Who's we?"

"Lissy. She's right here."

"Stay put. I'll be home as soon as George and I lock up. I don't like the look of this storm." Pop hesitated. "But I'm really glad you two are spending time together." The phone clicked and Kela hung up the receiver.

"Pop is coming," Kela said as she grabbed two towels from the closet and gave one to her friend.

"What are you going to tell him?"

Kela didn't answer. Instead she went into her room and opened a dresser drawer. She pulled out a dry T-shirt and shorts for herself and tossed some clothes to Lissy.

"Nothing right now," Kela said.

Lissy frowned.

Kela wanted to say more, but a deep tiredness overcame her. Of course she wasn't making sense. Nothing made sense.

They dried off in silence, peeling off shoes and socks and swapping wet clothes for dry.

"So, we're learning a new song in choir practice,"

Lissy said at last. "I have the solo."

"It's about time." Kela grinned. "Sister Evers didn't give it to Merlie again?"

"Sadly, no." Lissy sighed and put on her best tragic expression. "Unfortunately, she's visiting her family in the States for the summer."

"I'm glad you finally got a chance to solo," Kela replied. "You're a much better singer."

"I don't know about that."

"Look, you're great at two things," Kela said to her friend. "Words and music. Trust me."

Lissy smiled and Kela felt a tiny piece of her old life fit back into place. She had missed this easy banter with her friend.

The front door jiggled.

"I'm here," Pop called, knocking on the door to Kela's room. She opened it to let him in. Tall and dark-skinned like her, Pop dropped some of his gear from the dive shop in the hall.

"I should take you back to your grannie, Lissy. I'm sure she's worried about you out in this weather," he said. "We had to cancel our dives for this afternoon. Are you ready?"

"Thank you, Mr. Hendy," Lissy said quietly. "I just need to collect my clothes." Pop had told her she could call him by his first name long ago instead of Mr. Boxhill, his and Kela's last name. Lissy did, but her grandmother still insisted she add the "Mr."

"Go ahead," Pop said with a smile. "I'll wait in the kitchen."

Kela helped Lissy put her wet things into an old shopping bag. As Lissy turned toward the door, Kela grabbed her hand.

"Please don't say anything about the box," she said.

Lissy stared at her for a moment, then silently walked to the other room.

"I'll be back as quick as I can," Pop said to Kela. "The storm is getting bad."

Kela nodded and hugged a towel to her shivering body. Lissy shot a puzzled look at her before she walked with Pop to the truck. Kela soon heard it rumble away.

Dim light flickered in Kela's room. The storm thundered outside, and she hoped they wouldn't lose power.

Kela glanced at the turquoise picture frame that sat on her nightstand. Their trip to the Barrow Nature Park, lush with St. Rita's flora and fauna. Mum had leaned in to kiss her forehead, her dark locs tickling Kela's cheeks. In her dreams, she could still feel the warmth of that kiss on her skin.

She stood over the canvas bag.

She imagined explaining to her father that she had broken a cardinal rule. She had taken something from a protected site. He wouldn't care that it had been on land instead of underwater. As a dive instructor, he drilled that rule into tourists on each trip out on their boat. If it was important to him that she not remove shells from the beach, what would he think of this? A sick feeling churned in her stomach.

Kela shut her bedroom door. The tall hanging mirror banged against the wood. She kicked her wet clothes out of the way and craned to look at her sore knee.

She dotted it with ointment from the medicine cabinet and put a bandage on her scraped skin. The wind and slapping rain faded, like the world had decided to turn down its volume. Then she heard it.

The hum.

Picking up her bag, Kela sat on her bed. Taking a slow breath, she put her hand inside. A stabbing pain pierced her finger and she yanked her hand back out. A ragged splinter cut deep into her skin. She winced as she dug it out, then sucked her finger to stop the throbbing pain.

She peeked into the bag. The tumble down to the cave floor had damaged the box. Sharp fragments of wood jutted from one side. She twisted off the most finger-hungry pieces, then gingerly lifted out the box. The spongy wood slid beneath her fingers, and her heart ratcheted. Water sloshed. She pushed and pried, but no matter what she did, the lid stayed shut.

Kela wondered if the box had come from a shipwreck. Miss Inniss said that in the old days, the sea had become angry at the merchants who'd grown rich on the backs of the Africans dragged across the ocean against their will. Storm after storm often battered the islands and ports, and St. Rita's waters bore the scattered bones of several trading ships from long ago.

Currents were strong. Tossed in the ocean, the box may have tumbled for ages.

Thinking about shipwrecks reminded her of her mother. Mum might have known a story about old boxes hidden in the sea. It had been her job to collect stories, mysterious and magical, from all around the islands.

Mum's great-grannie had been a storyteller. Just like Miss Inniss. And like Lissy would be someday. She had once told Mum about a girl, a long-long-ago aunt, who'd been swept away by the sea and lost forever. When Grannie Montrose died, there was no one to keep the family stories except Mum. She had made it her life's work to save them.

Guilt still pinched. It was a job Kela hadn't appreciated. No matter how hard she wished, she couldn't take back what she had said to Mum. The slamming front door and the echo of her words, "I hate you," hung in the air. She couldn't jam the replay of that last morning with her mother any more than she could stop the heavy tightness in her chest.

So what did it matter?

Kela stuffed the box back into the canvas satchel. Her fingertips tingled. She couldn't fool herself. It did matter. Something inside the box had called to her. Led her to its hiding place deep in that cave. But why? She glanced at her bag.

Whatever was inside better be worth the trouble she would be in if Pop found out.

CHAPTER 5

Under the Pier

Pop returned before the worst of the storm hit. Windows rattled through the night, and he and Kela decided to keep each other company. She curled up on the thread-worn couch and Pop stretched out on the floor next to her, his too-big feet poking out from his blankets. But she couldn't sleep. The mystery of the box and everything that had happened swirled in her brain.

Kela got up and retrieved an old book tucked on a shelf. She turned on the lamp and sat cross-legged with the book in her lap.

It was a collection of Caribbean folktales that Mum used to read to her at bedtime. The faded blue fabric of the cover felt soft and warm beneath her fingers. She flipped carefully through its pages and smiled. "The Race Between Toad and Donkey." The story had made her laugh when she was little. Toad agreed to race Donkey to win a prize from the king. Though Donkey boasted of his speed, Toad tricked him by placing his own children behind each mile-post of the racecourse. Every time Donkey thought he was ahead, one of Toad's children jumped out and yelled:

"Jin-ko-ro-ro, Jin-kok-kok-kok."

Donkey mistook them for Toad and ran faster. Eventually, poor Donkey gave up because he thought there was no way he could win.

Other stories sent chills through Kela. She shivered as she thumbed past the tale of the Heartman, who lumbered through the night dragging his bag of beating children's hearts.

She finally turned to a story she knew by heart. One Mum had told her so many times as they picked their way along the beach looking for sea glass. As she read, Kela could almost hear the easy lilt in Mum's voice rising through the words.

It is said that when the seafolk first fanned their tails, the sea gathered them close. "Children, all of my waters are yours, but beware of land walkers. Stay in the cradle of my waves, far from the harm they might bring you." But her children did not listen. They were stubborn like the sea.

One daughter loved to watch the ships of men. With black locs that trailed like the tentacles of an anemone, she swam alongside and marveled. Soon, one land walker caught her eye, a captain. A terrible storm battered his ship, but he refused to leave the helm and was swept into the sea. The sea woman calmed the waves and the captain survived. She swam him to the shore, but he refused to let her return to the sea. His people dragged her to land and put her in a cage. She cried to be let go, but they only laughed and marveled at her tail. She soon died of a broken heart, longing for her sea home. Her mother and sisters cried in their grief. Their tears shimmered in the water and turned to glass. Salt and light, fragments of broken hearts. Mermaids' tears.

Kela closed the book and leaned back. She pictured the seafolk crying in despair and their beautiful tears washing to shore. Love and loss bound together.

Pop stirred on the floor. "What are you doing?" he murmured.

"Just reading," Kela replied.

He glanced at the book's cover and chuckled. "Those again? I'd have thought you'd be tired of that book."

"No." Kela lay down again, pulling her blanket high.

Pop used to tease Mum about whether she believed in the folktales she studied. She teased him right back. Her mother was a scholar and dutifully recorded what she was told by the people she interviewed. But sometimes . . . Mum talked about the stories like they were true.

And Kela? She didn't know what to think.

Even still, as the storm hammered the house, she was secretly glad Pop had insisted on staying close. Kela closed her eyes and drifted into a restless sleep.

When she woke, the room was empty, but Kela could hear Pop in the shower. She moved quickly, hoping to leave before he could stop her. She pulled her braids into a ponytail and put on her sneakers. Grabbing the canvas bag that she had hidden under her bed, Kela scribbled a quick note for Pop and left it on the kitchen table before she slipped silently out of the house.

Morning sun spun a brightness that fell numb on her bare brown arms. Baytown's narrow streets were littered with trash and debris, a sharp contrast to the beauty of yesterday's walk on the beach with Lissy. The storm's blows were as hard as they were unexpected, leaving the islanders of St. Rita with questions but no answers. Kela had no answers either, not even for herself.

The box banged against her side as she picked her way through the mess as quickly as she could. A familiar feeling loomed, like walking a tightrope. Breathe. Balance. Focus. Routines—the beach, the dive shop, crafting—kept her from falling into the swell of grief that lurked below. People watched, so part of the show required smiling. Kela tried not to worry anyone, especially Pop.

"Mornin', Kela. Such a mess, eh?"

Kela jumped. She hadn't noticed Mr. Bannister, his back bent as he piled cardboard into a wheelbarrow in front of his store. The red awning above his door sagged with storm water and a jagged crack fractured one of his windows.

"Good morning," Kela said. "Sorry for your troubles." Mangoes, papayas, ackees, and other produce crowded plastic bags, waiting for dry boxes.

"Ah, Miss Inniss sent Lissy down to help me. You just missed her." Removing his green summer cap, he mopped his sparse hair with a kerchief. "I don't see you two together much. Used to be thick as thieves."

Of course the grocer would notice. Everyone had. Even Kela half expected to see Lissy laughing at her side like she did when she had a joke to tell Kela.

Not anymore. But that was Kela's choice, and it hurt.

"I'm heading to see her now," Kela lied.

"Ah, that's good. Take care," Mr. Bannister said kindly as he returned to his work.

Kela skirted other storefronts, and despite what she had told the grocer, she scooted past Miss Inniss's familiar shop on the corner as well. Pop. Lissy. She didn't want to talk to anyone right now, except maybe Mum.

Salt hung in the damp air as Kela tightened her grip on her canvas bag. Fishing boats leaned along the docks, lines tangled and low in the water. Even their paint, a rainbow palette of Caribbean shades, looked beaten.

She needed to examine the box again, and she could think of only one place that was safe.

Foam lapped her toes as she walked the water's edge. On the hill above her, Baytown Harbor Resort bustled. Workers had quickly cleared this section of the boardwalk and beach closest to the hotel. Now joggers zigged through the wet sand and families loaded with towels and children made camp. She moved faster and kept her eyes focused ahead.

In the shade beneath the piers, she walked through the rough sand. On the other side of some large rocks, a flat slab squatted out of the sun and away from tourists. A good place to sit. She had spent a lot of time here since Mum died. Her quiet spot.

Vacationers always seemed in such a hurry, trying to cram as much as possible into their Four-Days-and-Three-Nights. St. Rita was her home though. On island-time, people didn't rush. What could be done today could just as easily be done tomorrow. At least that's what she used to think. Maybe the tourists weren't as foolish as she once thought.

Hidden from view, she lifted the bag from her shoulder and took the box out.

The possibility of magic existing had rarely entered her thoughts before now. In her sadness,

Kela wondered if Mum had led her to the box. She wanted to believe.

As Kela reached for the lid, the rough wood hummed under her touch and breathed an almost inaudible sigh.

The lock gave way as she lifted and the box swung its decrepit mouth wide.

How'd I do that? she wondered.

Briny seaweed was coiled inside to form a damp nest. The clammy strands slipped through her fingers as Kela pulled them out. A gleam of white flashed. She tugged more quickly, and when the muck was removed, she stared at what was left.

A comb.

It spanned the length of her palm and glinted white as bone. The upper tier was carved in an intricate openwork pattern with a border of zigzagging lines. The base bared thirteen sharp tines that mirrored the top arch. They reminded her of teeth.

As soon as she touched it, a strange sensation shot into her fingertips and snaked through her arm.

Around her, the pier vanished, and fractured images burst before her eyes. The looming outline of a boat overhead. A girl with brown skin and blue lips, ghostly in the watery light. A thin arm stretched beseechingly. A small light emerging from her mouth. A whisper, and a flash of gold.

The vision evaporated as quickly as it had appeared. Kela gasped and blinked. The girl had seemed slightly older than her, with clothes from a different time. Her plain cotton shift and bright orange madras skirt had billowed in the current, but it was her eyes Kela remembered most. Soft and brown, like her own.

Kela dropped the comb in the box and shut it, struggling to bring herself back to reality. She was sitting on a rock slab at the beach, under the pier, hugging her arms to her chest. She hoped to keep the strange dream away.

Magic. The only explanation that made sense. And not the kind in Mum's old book—the one of tricksters and talking animals. This was real. Her thoughts whirled as she tried to understand what she had seen. What if everything she had thought was wrong? Maybe she hadn't found the box.

Maybe it had found her.

Questions pushed forward. Who was the girl in orange madras? Was the whisper she'd heard a word? A name? What was the glint of gold?

Bigger problems lurked on the horizon. What

would Pop think if he found out? Divers and searchers were supposed to report valuable salvage items to the authorities. She wondered if she or Pop could go to jail. The weight of the box tripled in her lap.

Living on an island, there were always tales of the sea—deep and mysterious as the waters around St. Rita. Kela treasured them. Mum was gone, but the stories weren't. There was one other person who could help.

CHAPTER 6

The Storyteller

Kela threaded through the streets, her pulse racing to the rhythmic beats of soca music cascading through an open window. She tried to walk faster, but stalls of food packed the sidewalks. Breadfruit, plantains, coconuts. Fish cakes, cou cou, ackees. Every flavor of St. Rita was for sale.

Outside Baytown Corner Market, a crowd of women sat by the windows in painted chairs, laughing and chatting noisily. This was the way of the island. Storefronts were the town's front porches. A place out of the sun for people to gather, enjoy a refreshing drink, play a game, and talk.

Kela's heart skipped as she saw Lissy. Her instinct

to slide away tugged, like it had this morning, but she pushed it down.

"How you doing, girl?" Miss Inniss called out from a seat near the shop's door.

Her curly gray hair framed her face like a soft cap, and her wrinkles settled comfortably around her dimpled mouth.

"I'm okay." Kela shrugged. "Did the storm damage your shop?"

"Thank the Lord, no. I came in early to mop water and clean up."

Lissy side-eyed her from the far end of the row but stayed in her seat. Glancing away, Kela pulled up a crate close to Miss Inniss.

"The storm got me thinking about your stories."

Stories flowed freely around the island and Miss Inniss told them best. Kela and Lissy had spent hours listening together when they were younger.

"Which stories are on your mind?"

"The ones about the seafolk."

The old woman laughed. "Thinking about living in the sea?"

"No, it's just Mum used to . . ." Her voice trailed off.

Though Mum had taught Caribbean folklore at the local university, more than work had fueled her interest. "Listen," she had whispered in Kela's young ears. "The stories are part of us."

Miss Inniss patted Kela's knee.

"There are plenty of stories about seafolk. We just shared some tales a few days ago." Several women smiled and murmured in agreement when she gestured toward the group.

"Are there stories . . . about combs?"

"Oh yes . . . you got to beware of the seafolk and their combs," Miss Inniss said. "If I'm going to tell it, let us start the right way."

With the broad smile of a storyteller, she turned to the group.

"When I say Crick, you say Crack. Crick!"

"Crack!" said Kela and the group loudly. An island storyteller always began in this way. Mum said it was "call and response" and it came over with the enslaved Africans brought to work on the sugar plantations. It connected the teller and the listeners. She said a loud response showed the storyteller how much the listeners wanted the story.

Miss Inniss leaned forward and began. "This is a story. My grannie told me, and her grandmother told her. The seafolk have been round long before these islands were settled. Coming up out of the water at night, they sit on the rocks and twist their thick hair. Then, they tuck in their combs."

Kela's shoulders slumped—she was sure this would be a story she already knew. The movement did not pass Miss Inniss's notice.

"Oh, you think you've heard this before?" Miss Inniss said in mock offense. She let her voice drop. "Well, here's what you don't know. That comb is not just for their hair."

Unease skittered across the back of Kela's neck and down her spine.

Miss Inniss continued. "One time, an old fisherman came upon a sea woman sitting on a rock in the moonlight. Quick as a flash, she jumped back into the water. But she dropped her comb and the old man picked it up, because he knew it held powerful magic."

Some of the women chuckled, but then Lissy's quiet voice said, "People say you're lucky if you see the seafolk, but they can bring bad luck too." Her arms were crossed, but she frowned a little less. Lissy loved telling a good story as much as her grandmother did.

"Oh yes! Seafolk are a fickle bunch and can turn on a body in a second." Miss Inniss went on. "The old man called out to the sea woman, 'Mami Wata! Mami Wata!'

"And up she come," said Miss Inniss with a hop in her chair. Everyone laughed.

"When the old man showed the sea woman her comb, she asked, 'What you want from me?' He said, 'My wife is sick. I want the power to make her well.' The sea woman nodded and said, 'Rake me comb across the water. Then, you throw it back to me. You will have what you want.'

"The old man walked into the sea and raked that comb across the water," said Miss Inniss. "When he threw it back, the sea woman sank beneath the waves and disappeared. He thought for sure that he had been taken for a fool," she said.

"But lo and behold!" Miss Inniss sat up straight and opened her hands wide. "The old man woke up the next day with his brain full! He knew all types of herbs and healing spells and he was able to make his wife well."

Kela flexed her fingers, a phantom current still playing across her skin. "What would have happened if he hadn't thrown it back?"

"You don't want to get between a sea woman and her comb," Miss Inniss said. "If you do, a body should watch careful. Sure enough, that sea woman will come for what's hers."

Miss Inniss paused, then said, "Crick!"

"Crack!" responded the group. Kela's mouth felt dry around the word.

"The story is put on you," Miss Inniss said simply. Mum had told her that meant the listener had to decide what the story meant. She said stories lived in the ear of the hearer, not the teller.

What did it mean? Danger.

Someone, or something, had shaped the comb's sharp tines and polished them to cool smoothness. As Kela tried to understand the strange feelings that ran up and down her fingers, she looked at the facts.

She wished again that she could ask Mum about the box and the comb. As she thought about it more, she realized there was a way.

If she left now, she should be able to get home before Pop.

Kela scooted back her crate and stood up. While Miss Inniss laughed with the other ladies, Kela turned to the street and started walking. As she reached the end of the row of shops, she heard Lissy call out.

"Are you not talking to me again?" she asked.

Kela started to protest, but Lissy cut her off. "I saw you this morning. You walked right by the shop and didn't even stop. I kept your secret from your pop and Gran. I thought we were friends."

"We are friends," Kela said. The rebuke stung like a slap.

"Well, I don't like how you show it," Lissy said. Her chest heaved a little, but Kela could tell she was not as mad as before.

"Lissy, I'm sorry."

Lissy shifted and looked away at the beach.

"I could use your help," Kela said tentatively. "If you want to come with me."

Lissy looked at her suspiciously. "Does it have anything to do with that seafolk stuff you were asking Gran?"

"Yes—and Mum."

The expression on Lissy's face softened. "What do the seafolk have to do with your mum?"

"I'll tell you on the bus. Hurry up and tell your grannie you're going to be gone for a while."

Lissy hesitated a moment, then nodded. She ran over to her grandmother and said a few words, then dashed inside the shop.

Miss Inniss walked over to Kela while Lissy was inside the store.

"I'm happy to see you two talking," Miss Inniss said. "I know Lissy's been confused about why you stopped coming around."

Kela swallowed. In the spotlight of Miss Inniss's concern, she could only hang her head.

Somehow Miss Inniss gathered understanding from the unspoken words.

"You need to grieve in your own way. Lissy knows that too," she said. "Just try not to leave behind the people who care about you."

Kela dipped her head at the crinkled brown face of the woman who always produced the right words at the moment needed.

"Almost forgot," Miss Inniss said, her voice lighter. "I sold the last piece of your jewelry yesterday." Pulling a wrinkled envelope from her pocket, she handed it to Kela.

It held some bills and a few coins. Kela tucked it in her pocket.

"Thanks."

Miss Inniss swished her hand as if batting a fly. "Don't thank me. They sell themselves. Your talent amazes everyone."

"I'll bring something new later."

"More than fine, dear. I'll call your father to let him know you're going to town. He can also pick up some roti for dinner, all right? I made chicken and potato."

"Thank you," Kela said with a smile as Lissy returned.

The girls walked together toward the bus stop and Kela looked out over the rippling water. She wondered if there was some truth in the old tales. An icy fear crept over her.

Who or what might come for her?

CHAPTER 7
Call of the Comb

Crick.

Crack.

This is a story.

The comb reached across the waves. She felt the girl's trembling fingers wrapped tight around it. Magic tethered them now. When the sun drowned in the warm waters, Ophidia would come on tides of shadow.

How best to make the introduction? She narrowed her eyes as she swam.

Most humans needed to be convinced of her existence, and her beauty proved an effective tool with some. With others, her power tempted them.

The young accepted her without question and were ready to believe in things unseen. In miracles and magic. She believed they called it "faith."

But bargains struck with children were more complicated.

Ophidia dove deeper, leaving the warmth of the sun for the piercing chill of deep waters. Her pulse slowed as gloom gnawed the edges of the shrinking ball of light from above. She needed to prepare.

Children wished from the heart, and their trust that magic fixed all things made them wish deeply. But the truth was that magic could not fix all.

She had granted some truly foolish wishes in her existence. Warned of the risks but blinded by their desires, most humans did not listen.

At last, Ophidia entered the mouth of the cave. Rocks jutted like rotten teeth. Much time had passed since she'd been here last, and she had hoped she would never return. To speak to this girl, Ophidia needed what this place offered. A way to bridge the sea with the world above. Here she would make her bargain—offering a wish in exchange for her comb's return.

If she did not regain it, this would be the last wish she would grant.

Ophidia settled in her dark place to wait. Tonight.

She would contact this new wishmaker and offer her the world. How much would it cost for the girl to yield her heart's secrets? Only the sea knew.

Crick.
Crack.
The story is put on you.

CHAPTER 8
Beneath the Surface

Brown pods rattled above as Kela and Lissy walked under the shade of the shak shak trees. They arrived at the bus stop, and before long, the bus to Queensland pulled up and they got on.

As the bus bounced and bumped, Kela told Lissy everything. About the hum, the vision, and the shock still tingling in her arm. She opened the box and Lissy hesitantly ran her fingers over the cold white of the comb's surface.

"Did it happen right away?"

"Yeah." When nothing happened after another moment, Kela added, "It's all right." Lissy withdrew her hand. Like the hum before, the electric jolt and the vision that accompanied it seemed only for Kela.

She put the box away and told Lissy about her plan.

Queensland reigned as the island's main port and hotspot for tourists and city culture. St. Rita College, where Mum had worked, was one of many institutions the city claimed. But they weren't going there.

During her vision, she remembered thinking the box had come from a shipwreck. Mum had collected dozens of stories of ships that had sunk off the island's coast. Everything had been locked away after Mum died. If Kela could get to her files, they might hold a clue to her strange hallucination and the spidery prickle that chased up her arm.

On the winding road, Kela gripped the window edge with one hand and clutched her satchel with the other. Her sweaty palms slid along the smooth aluminum as cars and other buses zipped around hairpin turns. She blinked away the image of rain, Mum's red umbrella, and her car flying off the road, and instead focused on the music pumping from the bus driver's radio.

The St. Rita Museum and Historical Society overlooked the southern coast, its stone lookout tower a reminder of its days as a military fort. She had come here often with Mum to work in the archives or to visit Mum's friend Joyce, who was a curator. They had gone to college together and could ramble on and on about random bits of history. Kela never thought she'd miss that, but she did.

She remembered working on her jewelry among the dusty bookcases while Mum pored over her notes and recordings. Lost in stories.

Climbing the cobbled steps, Kela and Lissy rehearsed what they planned to say.

Inside the arched doors, the girls stopped at the reception desk.

"Good morning," Kela said, rubbing her hand along the side of her shorts. The young woman behind the desk raised her eyes from the book she was reading and pushed up her glasses.

"Can I help you?"

"May we use the bathroom?"

"Uh . . ." the woman said with hesitation. "Are you by yourselves?"

Kela looked at Lissy, who crossed her legs and put on a pleading expression.

"My father's waiting outside. My friend really has to go!"

"Fine. Just go!" The receptionist pointed down the hall. "Past the first exhibit hall and by the water fountain on the right."

The girls thanked her and dashed in the direction she had pointed.

When they were out of sight, Kela had to suppress a giggle. "I thought you might pee yourself for real," she whispered.

"Never doubt my acting skills," Lissy said with a dramatic swish of her hand. "It's part of being a good storyteller. I was afraid it might be someone who'd recognize you."

"I think it'll be easier if we stay undercover."

The girls hurried down the hall. The sign by the first exhibit hall read "Natural History Wing: Prehistoric Fossils." Glancing in, Kela saw the room was full of old bones and teeth. A prickle ran across her neck. They continued past the water fountain and the bathroom, then crept down a set of stairs to the lower level.

It was quiet. A place for dusty old volumes and items not on display.

They finally stopped in front of a door labeled "Private Archives."

"It's in here," Kela said to Lissy. There was a keypad on the lock and Kela hoped that her mother's access code still worked. She punched in the numbers she had watched Mum push so many times whenever Kela went with her to work: 7-8-1-3. The seconds stretched forever, then the small red light turned green and was followed by a sharp *click*.

Kela quickly opened the door, and she and Lissy scooted inside and shut it behind them.

The automatic lights flickered on and Kela pulled the shade on the door's window. The private archives towered with long rows of boxes and files. Each metal shelf told what types of materials were kept in the section: maps and charts, genealogical records, property deeds, letters and manuscripts, and so on.

Kela walked to the section labeled "Oral History Collections." She knew what she was looking for.

"Here," she said, beckoning Lissy closer.

They stopped in front of a row of boxes labeled "Folklore Archives—Boxhill."

"These are Mum's notes," Kela said quietly. "If she recorded any stories about combs and the sea-folk, they would be here. We could find out where it came from."

"Where should we start?" Lissy said, looking nervously at the stacks of dusty boxes.

"When I came with Mum, she showed me how

each box was organized by topic. Last time she was filing records about duppies." Kela peered at the neat labels on the boxes. "Here! This is what she was working on," she said, pointing to a box labeled "Duppies, Jumbies, and Spirit Tales." She walked down the row. "We just need to find one related to the sea or seafolk."

The girls spread out and studied labels, crouching or stretching to read them. Lissy whispered, "Kela, I think I found something."

Kela hurried over and looked at the box in front of Lissy. "Seafolk Legends and Sightings." They pulled it from the shelf and carried it to a table. Kela lifted the lid.

The box was an odd collection of papers, notebooks, cassette tapes, and other artifacts. Kela breathed and sat down.

"Are you all right?" Lissy asked.

"Next to me and Pop, these stories were what Mum cared about most."

"You don't have to do this. We can leave, if you want."

Kela took the old wooden box out of her bag and set it on the table. The rusty keyhole seemed to blink.

"No, I have to do this."

She pulled a stack of notebooks from the archive box and opened the first. Mum's even script flowed across the page. *June 2015—Interview with Miss Henrietta Maloney*. Kela traced her fingers over the words and imagined her mother's voice. *Rockview, St. Rita. I sat down with Miss Maloney, age eighty-one, to record a story about singing heard from the sea . . .*

Kela blinked fast to make the words stop blurring. Focus, she ordered herself.

She began to flip through the pages. Names, dates, places, and stories. Many, many stories. Some were familiar, like the ones in her book of folktales. Others were different. They described heart-aching songs from the waves that lured fishermen to their deaths. Mysterious lights in the water. If she found a mention of combs, it was only in passing.

As Kela pushed away notebooks and pulled out others, she grew frustrated. She glanced at the old box. It stared silently, refusing to reveal any clues.

Finally, Kela slammed shut the last notebook. Reading Mum's words had left her heart raw and her body drained. She turned to tell Lissy they should go, but her friend had sat up.

"Kela, look at this."

She slid over to see what Lissy was reading.

Kela picked up a photocopy of an old handwritten letter. The print was small and had curly letters that she had to squint to read. She noticed the date: September 1667.

Dearest Mary,

Providence has enabled me to write to you again. A tempest ravaged the fair island of St. Rita, leaving few houses and sugar mills standing. The frightful storm rose without warning and left the coast in devastation. Eight fully laden vessels ran aground, their cargo of sugar a loss. The wretched wails of women and children echoed in the shambles of Queensland and other ports. Though my parish is no more, I and dear Sarah do what we can to offer comfort to those in despair. The need is great. Coffee, sugarcane, and other provisions were destroyed and earnest pleas for aid go out lest famine take hold. Havoc and ruin surround the inhabitants of St. Rita—governor, plantation owners, labourers, slaves, and freedmen. May the Lord have mercy on us all.

Your loving brother,
William

"What's the difference between laborers and freedmen?" asked Kela.

"Freedmen were Black people who were free. Grannie told me there weren't many back then, but some people were born free or sometimes they could work to buy their own freedom," Lissy replied.

"I don't understand," Kela said. "Why is this letter stored with stories about the seafolk? They're not even mentioned."

"It reminds me of the storm last night," Lissy said slowly. "Maybe . . . someone thought seafolk caused this hurricane in the 1600s." Kela frowned, but before she could interrupt, Lissy laid her hand on the letter. "And your mum must have thought this was important."

"I don't know," Kela said. She slumped in her chair. "I feel like we're missing something."

Lissy glanced at the clock and said, "We've been here for a while. We should probably leave."

Kela took Mum's notebooks, the letter, and some other loose papers and slid them into her bag with the wooden box. She and Lissy put everything else back in the archive box and returned it to the shelf. At the door, Kela turned out the lights and peeked under the window shade. The hallway was empty.

She cracked the door open, then she and Lissy slipped out. They ran down the hall and turned the corner to the stairs, but their way was blocked.

"I found them," the security guard said into his radio.

CHAPTER 9
Song of the Sea

Crick.

Crack.

This is a story.

The sea woman had not always possessed a soul.

From the first tides, seafolk had lived and died. Three hundred years they swam before returning to the white foam of the waves. Through magic, they learned they could extend their lives.

As she rested in the cradle of the tide, Ophidia's mind drifted. Back and back and back.

She had heard the incompatible sound of water fighting against air. Would she have the strength to watch someone die if it meant she could live forever?

Ophidia pumped her tail hard. Souls could be salvaged, but she must be there at the right moment. Like the brilliant fireflies that glowed above the surface, the soul would float from the human's mouth, then vanish to the other side—unless she could trap it in a soul cage. She had brought one, crudely made with her own hands, but it would serve. She would live an immortal life, as long as she kept it hidden and safe.

This was the way it always had been. If Ophidia wanted the immortality of the seafolk, she had to take a soul. She refused to hunt and lure like her siren sisters, who valued their own lives over all others. She only looked for those whose fates were sealed.

Ophidia approached the figure struggling in the water. The outline of a small skiff loomed above. A wooden fishing pole sank slowly into the deep. The sea woman had been told what to do. The human's jerky motions slowed, and the end drew near.

Then, the girl turned.

Her brown skin paled in the shallow light and her lips were already blue. Her eyes widened. Always the same. A pendulum of fear, then hope, then fear.

This girl was dying—and soon Ophidia would have a second life.

But she felt the thing she had been warned against. Pity.

Ophidia repeated her mother's words. "Humans aren't to be trusted. Humans only take."

The girl's eyes closed and her mouth parted. A glow like a light deep in a cave floated closer. In a moment, it would be hers.

But who did this girl love? Did anyone wait for her back on the land? Unwanted questions peppered the sea woman's thoughts.

"She will bring you sorrow, daughter," the sea warned.

Ophidia reached out her hand.

Just before the light escaped, she closed the girl's mouth. In a spray of salty sea, she pushed the limp body back into the boat.

The girl spewed a stomachful of water. Ophidia shrank back.

When she stopped retching, the girl scanned the ocean and her eyes found Ophidia.

"You saved me."

Instinct pulled Ophidia toward the safety of the sea, and she backed away.

"Don't go!"

The sea woman hesitated. Her heart beat fast.

"Thank you."

Ophidia swam to the boat.

In the cold waters of the present, shadows and dreams troubled Ophidia's mind as she tossed in her sleep.

She will bring you sorrow, daughter.

Her mother had been right.

Crick.

Crack.

The story is put on you.

CHAPTER 10
Truth and Consequences

"What were you girls doing down here?" the guard asked sternly.

"I'm sorry. We were looking for the bathroom and got lost," Kela said quietly.

"The receptionist said she let you go to the bathroom almost an hour ago. Where have you been?"

Kela tensed and looked at Lissy. Her friend's face was frozen in panic.

"Kela? Is that you?" Staccato footsteps clipped down the corridor and the girls turned. A tall woman with close-cropped hair approached.

"Joyce!" Kela exclaimed. Her face filled with relief at seeing Mum's old friend.

"What are you doing here?"

The security guard looked stunned. "Ms. Callender, do you know these girls? I was about to escort them to the security office."

"I was actually here to see you, Joyce," Kela said hurriedly. "I thought I'd show Lissy where you work."

"That's sweet!" Joyce said. She turned to the guard. "It's fine, Joe. I'll take care of them." The guard made a sour face but turned and clomped up the stairs.

"It's so good to see you!" Joyce said, giving Kela a tight hug. "How are you?"

"Okay." She hadn't talked to her mother's friend since the funeral, and the thought made a hard lump rise in her throat. "Thanks for seeing us."

"You can stop by anytime," Joyce said emphatically. She pointed to her wire crocheted necklace with blue beads and tiny sea glass charms that sparkled. "What do you think?"

"It looks great on you."

"I get so many compliments when I wear your pieces. I hope you're still making them. Believe me, a future in jewelry design is yours if you want it."

Kela's faced warmed with the compliment.

"So, what's going on?" Joyce's face creased in concern. "Do you need anything?"

"I found something and wanted to learn more about it."

Lissy looked at Kela with wide eyes, but Kela put her hand on Lissy's arm to reassure her friend.

"Sounds interesting," Joyce said. "Let's find a place to talk."

She motioned Kela and Lissy to follow her upstairs and opened the door to a narrow conference room. Sunlight streamed in from a large window, and the three settled at one end of a long polished table. Kela took the wooden box out of her bag and passed it to Joyce.

"And where did you find this?" She studied the box with interest.

"Diving with Pop down at Hastings Point. I picked it up from the seafloor." The lie rolled easily off Kela's tongue and she glanced sideways at Lissy to play along.

"This looks recent," she said, poking at the splintered wood along the box's edge. "Do you know what happened?"

"Uh, no," Kela replied, shifting uncomfortably in her chair.

"Hmm . . ." Joyce looked at Kela with a slight frown. "You know, you probably shouldn't have removed this. There are some strict guidelines for collecting off the coast."

"But there are exceptions," Kela said quickly. "If I had left it, the current could have pulled it out to deeper water. Then it might have been lost forever."

"You have a point," Joyce said. "Have you opened it?"

"Yes," Kela said. "The box stuck at first but then it just opened."

The curator lifted the lid and her eyes widened. "Beautiful." She peered more closely.

"It looks old. Do you know where it might have come from?" Kela asked.

Joyce got up and pulled a pair of white gloves and a magnifying glass from a side table drawer. She shook her head as she turned the comb over in her gloved hands, tracing her fingers along the tines and wavy lines.

"This reminds me of some African combs. It looks hand-carved from ivory, perhaps bone. The zigzag pattern is common. It's thought to be a reminder to 'follow the path of the ancestors,' which may be difficult. These open carvings are truly exquisite, though." Joyce picked up the magnifying glass and examined the comb more closely. Looking at the back, she said, "There seems to be a symbol or letter carved at the base of the comb. It's hard to make out. Maybe a letter *M*? It could be the artist's mark."

Turning the comb back over, Joyce frowned. "Hmm, there's a hairline crack running along the middle of the top arch. Hard to know if that's from the recent damage or not. It would be best to avoid handling it anymore. I'd hate for such a beautiful piece to break."

Kela could still see the box tumbling out of her grip and flying through the air, could still hear the *thwack* of its side hitting the coral. She shook her head to stay focused.

Joyce put the magnifying glass down. "We don't hold anything like this in our collection." She considered Kela with a curious expression. "What are you and your father planning to do with it? It's a remarkable find."

Kela shifted again and shrugged.

"I'm not an expert in this area, but I can tell you that this find is valuable. Knowing the history of the island, I can only guess that it came from a merchant vessel. Maybe one of the ships that wrecked back in the 1700s, maybe older than that. I've never seen anything like it, and the possibility of researching it would grab any museum's attention, including ours."

Joyce sat up and glanced toward the door.

"By the way, where is your father? Why didn't he come with you?"

Kela scratched her arm. "He got tied up at the shop, and I told him that Lissy and I could visit you on our own—anyway, it's been so long since we've seen each other."

Joyce smiled sadly and relaxed.

"I'm glad you came," she said, patting Kela's hands. "And you too, Lissy." Joyce sat back. "Unfortunately, you need to tell your father that he's walking on shaky legal ground. The government could claim ownership of your comb based on cultural heritage. Even though where you found it was not a protected wreck or archaeological site, it may fall under the laws governing the protection of underwater history. Has he filed a claim yet?"

"Not yet," Kela said. "He wanted to talk to someone who knew about this sort of stuff first."

Joyce glanced at the comb, still in her hand, then studied Kela.

"It sounds as if your father is rather busy. If you'd like, I'd be happy to take care of this. I can't say that I feel comfortable leaving something so valuable and fragile in the hands of children."

Kela swallowed hard. "Oh no. Pop knows how careful we are. I'll tell him what you said about filing a claim with the Ministry of Culture."

Joyce held her gaze, then finally nodded. She carefully put the comb back into the box, closed the lid, and slid it back to Kela.

"Well, I would tell him to do that immediately. If I were you, I'd lock it up somewhere safe for now. That's a work of art and really should be on display in a museum."

"Understood. Thanks."

"Kela . . . this puts me in an awkward position," Joyce said as she removed the white gloves. "As a curator, I'm legally bound to report knowledge of the removal of culturally significant artifacts." She leaned forward. "Your father will do the right thing, but eventually I may need to call the Ministry."

A sinking dread filled Kela as she listened to Joyce.

"I'll tell him."

Kela and Lissy followed Joyce back to the hallway and upstairs to the front door. Joyce gave Kela another tight hug, then the girls went outside and walked toward the bus stop.

"Kela, why did you tell her you found it diving?"

"I couldn't tell her the truth. What she said was bad enough. Imagine if she knew I took it from the coral reserve?"

What had she done? Kela knew a little more than

before, but now Joyce might call the government about her and Pop having such a valuable object. Pop might end up in trouble—because of her.

She and Lissy didn't talk much once they got on the bus. The sky turned a hazy shade of coral and pink as the tired sun burned lower. Riding the speeding bus back to Baytown, Kela wondered where the truth lay. Could the comb belong to the seafolk like Miss Inniss said, or did it wash away from a shipwreck? She wondered what the letter *M* on the comb meant.

Whatever the answers, Kela was sinking deeper into trouble.

CHAPTER 11
The Last Day

Pop brought George home for dinner. Her father's partner was the closest thing Kela had to an uncle. At the shop, he would tug playfully on her braids, then pretend he was busy with something else when she turned around. She had stopped falling for that when she was three.

The rotis Miss Inniss had made were ready as promised, warm and stuffed with curried chicken and potatoes. George tried to crack his usual jokes. They mostly fell between bites of silence.

"Thank you," Kela said, when George gave her the fried plantains he had brought. Deliciously painful, they rolled salty-sweet on her tongue but picked at her memories like carrion.

"Tell you what, I'll make plantains for dinner. Your favorite," Mum had said on that last day.

Rain was falling hard outside, and Mum's red umbrella leaned by the door, ready to whisk her away from the storm inside the house.

"You promised me you would take me to the craft store." Kela threw the words like darts. "You said you'd make time."

Her mother's new job—curating a collection of stories from around the islands—had turned Kela's life upside down. Mum loved it, but deadlines pushed aside time together at the beach, and extra chores kept Kela from her jewelry-crafting.

"That's not fair," her mother said. "This hasn't been an easy transition, but we're all responsible and need to pitch in to make it work."

When Kela didn't answer, Mum walked over and stroked her hair. The familiar gesture made Kela's eyes sting, but she refused to look up.

"This conversation has to wait until I get home." Mum shoved files and notebooks into her overstuffed bag. "I can't talk right now."

Kela laid her head on her arms. "I hate you."

Mum closed her eyes before kissing Kela on the head. She grabbed her umbrella and hustled into the rain. The door slammed.

Later, Kela stared at an ant crawling across the kitchen floor as a constable explained how her mother's car lost control on the wet, narrow curve to Queensland. As Pop clutched his head and bawled without shame, her eyes followed the tiny ant. Carrying a crumb twice its size, it never stopped or seemed to miss a step, following an invisible trail back to the anthill outside.

Three months had gone, but still Kela resisted her mother's death. For a while, Pop seemed to be in the same fog that engulfed her. He stopped going to work, letting George run their business on his own, and hardly left his bedroom.

After the accident, people moved around her house like phantoms. Their presence wasn't as real as her pain. Still, they brought meals, stayed with Kela when her father returned to work, cleaned the house, and did anything else they could to help. Mum always said that St. Ritans showed their love with their hands.

When the visitors retreated, the silence in the house grew louder. Pop put on a positive face, but when he thought she slept, the thin walls didn't keep her from hearing his grief. She cried quietly with him.

Kela marched along, carrying her own burden,

following the trail of her old routines. A knot burned in her throat every time she let herself remember Mum, but she realized it also burned when she didn't remember. She didn't know which was better.

Miss Inniss made sure Kela ate and offered a ready ear if she wanted to talk. Lissy came around at first, but what Kela wanted most was to be alone. Despite everyone's efforts to prop up the fragments of her life, the truth wouldn't change. Her mother died and wasn't coming back.

After dinner, Pop stretched back in his chair with a satisfied grin.

"Ah! Miss Inniss knows my weakness. All those ladies can throw down in the kitchen. It's enough to keep me coming to church every Sunday."

"I'm with you, man," George said. "I've got to run, but let me take home a plate." Kela wrapped a dish with a little of everything and gave it to him. "Thanks, Kela. See you tomorrow, Hendy!"

After George left, Pop settled in front of the television to watch highlights from the cricket championships. He groaned when he read the standings. Baytown had made it to the finals against Queensland, but the other team had fought back and pulled ahead. More than parish pride was at stake.

"I can't believe I took up George's wager," Pop

said. "He'll be boasting all week if Queensland wins." Kela could imagine that easily.

She leaned against her father and picked at the thoughts spinning since that afternoon. Spending hours by the sea and listening to stories. It had meant so much to her mother, and those memories filled Kela's childhood. But she wasn't a child anymore.

The secret of the comb and the threat of trouble for her father weighed heavily on her mind too. Finally, the question that swelled inside her burst out.

"Why don't you ever talk about Mum?"

Pop pushed himself up, his brow furrowed. Kela focused on her hands and not on her father's intent face.

"You never even mention her name." The words came fast and she worried they would stick in her throat.

Pop's voice tightened. "I—I didn't want to make things harder for you and I thought it would be too painful."

She had done the same thing, Kela realized. Guilt had also kept her silent. She would've given anything if she could change what she had said to Mum.

"It's like we're pretending," Kela said, trying to avoid his gaze. "Like we think not talking about it is going to make it go away."

Pop rubbed his hands together, as if massaging feeling into them.

"You're right," he said, sagging back into the couch. "Miss Inniss told me I had 'hard ears' for not listening to her." The pain in his brown eyes vibrated in his voice.

"Sometimes, I think it's my fault," she said. Her throat felt thick.

"Do you mean the accident?" Pop asked.

"She worked so much and everything changed, so I got angry." Kela picked at a thread on the couch. "Before she left, I said—I hated her."

Speaking this secret brought relief, but Kela couldn't bear to meet Pop's eyes.

Pop's strong arms wrapped around her and she rested her head on his chest. Her bottom lip pressed in as she tried to control her quavering breaths.

"Your mum knew you loved her," Pop said, "and she loved us too. It's not your fault, and nothing good can come from blaming yourself."

Having the words out of her head and in the open consoled her, but she didn't agree with her father. She'd still do anything to take them back.

"If anything, it's my fault you've struggled. Not talking wasn't right and I'm going to do better." Lifting her face, he said, "If we're going to start talking about Mum, you can't avoid discussing some other things too." He raised an eyebrow at her.

Her heart caught in her throat. Did he know about the comb? She didn't want to tell him that secret yet.

"Lissy," he said.

Kela sighed and remembered that he had talked to Miss Inniss that evening.

"Things are better, but I don't always know what to say to her," Kela said, her words tumbling hard like stones. "She has a family. I don't want her feeling sorry for me." Her voice was muffled in the folds of her father's shirt.

"Your family is here. Me, Miss Inniss, Lissy, and George."

That was true, but she wanted back what she had had.

Later, the conversation with her father replayed in her head as she got ready for bed. As she wrapped her braids in a scarf, a quiet knock sounded at the door.

"Come in."

His face didn't look as tight as before, but for a moment, Kela saw her own tired sadness etched in the crinkles around his brown eyes. He hesitated.

"Believe me, I don't want to get out of bed my own self some days. It's hard now, but we need to stick together."

The words were familiar, but her father's expression was sincere. He wanted to keep his promise of "doing better." She hugged him tight, but guilt at what she still hid burned inside her.

"Miss Inniss tells me you've made quite a bit of money with your jewelry so far," he said. "I'll pay whatever you still need for the Creative Arts Program. Isn't the deadline coming up soon?"

Kela's walls rose, and she shook her head. Pop didn't understand.

"Why not?" he asked. "You have the talent and it's a great opportunity."

"I don't want to think about it now." She had promised she would go. If promises to the dead counted.

Kela meant it when she said she didn't know how to be around people anymore. How could she be with dozens of kids who were strangers, kids who didn't walk tightropes like she did, when she even had trouble around Lissy, her best friend?

"I won't pressure you. We have enough to think about," Pop said. He kissed her on the top of her head. "Let's talk about it later."

The door clicked behind him.

Kela turned off the light and got into bed. The mirror spilled moonlight onto her floor. As she burrowed into the softness of her blanket, the heavy sensation of sleep enveloped her. Mum, the stories, the comb. Quieting the thoughts in her head proved hard. As she sank into sleep, she imagined singing.

The sound of dripping water lulled her.

CHAPTER 12

The Other Side of the Mirror

Kela's eyes snapped open. Flickering shadows danced along the walls.

She swung her feet to the floor, gasped, and yanked them back. Icy water numbed her toes and her thoughts, flowing across her room and stranding her on a four-poster island. Below her, the glassy surface reflected the moon's light. A slow falling cascade echoed in the room and set the hairs on her neck straight up. *Dr-rop Dr-rip Rip.* The house slept in silence except for the phantom fall of water.

Easing her feet back down, she hop-stepped to the door, intending to wake her father. Her fingers stretched for the knob but stopped mid-reach.

The hanging mirror.

An undulating wall of water, it did not reflect her narrow face or long box braids. Instead, indistinct shapes moved behind a liquid veil. Water trickled down the frame to the floor.

Transfixed by its rolling surface, Kela stared. Its rise and fall was like a creature's restless breathing.

I must be dreaming.

Her mind refused to accept what her senses perceived, and instead her thoughts reeled with practical questions. Yet the tingle in her fingers dragged her toward the truth. Sweat clung to her palms.

She shook her head, trying to rattle the dream's hold. This can't be real . . . Fear bubbled in her throat. Kela swallowed it and stretched her hand again toward the knob.

But the mirror moved faster.

Water shot forward, crashing against her body and wrapping her tightly. Kela struggled but could not free herself from the watery shroud that pinned her arms and crept up her neck. As she sucked in a final breath of sweet air, water covered her mouth and nose. The sea lifted Kela off the floor and pulled her through the gaping mouth of the mirror.

On the other side of the nightmare, the sea let go. Panicked by the smothering dark that engulfed her, she cried out. Her hands flew to her mouth to stop the release of her last precious bubbles of air, but the choking spasm she expected didn't come. She could breathe. The rush of water through her nose and mouth was like air, and her body floated without effort.

Unlike the cold that had frozen her feet in the bedroom, the water on this side caressed her skin with warmth. The gentle swells pacified her jerky movements, like a stranger rocking a frightened child. She didn't dare trust the overture.

The bank of sand Kela descended onto was more like the white powder of the beach than the coarseness of the ocean bottom. She wiggled her toes to test it. Her room, her house, the street outside her window—gone; St. Rita did not exist here.

Instead, she was huddled in an underwater alcove. No clear source of light illuminated the space, but she could see. Water refracted the indistinct glow in strange ways as she blinked. Free of the scarf, her braids floated like sea fans and her nightgown billowed. Her heart pounded.

Immense shadows mimicked movement hidden just out of sight. A soft lilt of music grew louder, and an unearthly voice carried the rhythm and roll of steel drums.

A reckless curiosity gripped Kela and she propelled

herself toward the sound. With a small kick, her body sliced through the water. She eased around the corner, crouching, and with her senses alert.

A figure sat on a stone, her back turned. She was tall and lithe, and her black locs swirled in the current. Below the waist, her ebony skin transformed into brilliant scales of green and gold. A muscled tail flicked without concern.

The creature turned her head. Eyes. Snakelike and molten gold with black slits. The cold stare made Kela shrink.

The sea woman flashed sharp alabaster teeth, but that did not put Kela at ease. It was the smile of a predator.

"Who are you?" Kela asked, gripping the wall of the alcove.

The sea woman slid sinuously off the rock. Silver-flecked scales plated her chest and climbed to her neck.

"I am Ophidia." Her voice rose in a soft, musical cadence. Kela's eyes were drawn to her throat, and her heart stumbled. Around Ophidia's neck hung an exquisite shard of sea glass, the perfect shade of orange, blazing in the rayless current.

"How did I get here?" Kela's mouth sputtered the words as though from a rusty spigot.

"I could answer that, but it's not really the right question." Tinkling laughter filled the space.

"What is the right question?"

"Ask me why you are here."

"Why am I here?" The bubbling fear rose again.

"You have something of mine." The words dripped with accusation.

"The comb?" Kela faltered. "How did you know?"

"It calls to me and I am drawn by its touch."

Kela let go of the wall and clasped her arms tightly, feeling betrayed by her hands.

"Don't worry . . ." Ophidia continued. "I am willing to make a fair exchange for it. Then everyone will receive what they want."

"An exchange?"

"A trade. I will grant you a wish and you must give back what is mine." An agitated swish of her tail hinted at more beneath the sea woman's calm appearance. "That's a fair proposition, don't you think?"

"You're talking about real magic. This isn't a dream?"

"No. I am very real." Her tail swished again.

Kela thought for a moment. "Can I wish for anything?"

"That is my offer. It is one that many of your kind would envy."

To have anything she wanted? Unimaginable. Her pulse sped as she fixed on the one thing she wanted most.

"Before you accept, heed a warning," Ophidia said, her voice no longer light. "Magic always has a cost, and it can be dear. Dwell carefully on that. The stronger the magic you invoke, the deeper the consequence." Ophidia's eyes narrowed. "Foolish tears of regret cannot change your choice."

"Are there wishes you can't grant?" Kela asked. Ophidia must hear the *ta-ta-thump* of her skipping heart.

"All things are within my power if you are willing to pay the price." Ophidia reached to the seafloor, then extended her hand toward Kela. She held a pebble. "Imagine this is a wish dropped in a pool. A small stone creates small ripples, and dropping a larger stone creates larger ripples. The consequence of magic is in proportion to its strength."

Kela didn't understand the tangle of Ophidia's words, except for this: Her deepest desire could be hers . . . if she agreed to the price. How high would it be? But she already knew she would give anything.

"One more thing," Ophidia said. "Nothing can be created from nothing. Magic must be kept in balance. For something given, something must be lost."

"What will be lost?"

"Who knows?" Ophidia shrugged indifferently. "Magic is like water. It will follow the easiest path and find balance."

"What do I need to do?"

With a flick of her tail, the sea woman closed in, inches from Kela's face. The bottomless ink of her eyes swallowed all, and Kela jerked back at the suddenness.

"Rake my comb across the water and tell the sea what you want. It will be done." Her unblinking eyes held their gaze. "But if you fail to throw my comb back into the deep . . ." A threat coiled within Ophidia's voice. "I will drag you to the bottom of the waves."

The water, which had once embraced Kela, began to suffocate her. Her throat felt like cotton as she forced herself to swallow.

Danger loomed on all sides of this choice. She would be granted a wish, but there would be a consequence equal in size, and if she followed her heart, that consequence could be massive. And if she didn't return the comb? She didn't want to think about that.

Kela squirmed under Ophidia's scrutiny. As time ticked forward, her appearance softened, and her eyes burned gold again. Kela thanked whatever had brought the change.

"Do you accept my offer?" Ophidia said.

Kela rubbed the side of her neck, weighing the choices. Part of her knew that a right and a wrong existed, but this could make everything right. The way it should have been.

"I accept," she said, her voice carrying more strength than she felt.

The sea woman grasped Kela's hands, elongated fingers holding tight. Kela flinched in her cold grip.

"It is sealed, but know this. If I do not receive what is mine, I will come for you."

As soon as Ophidia released her, Kela backed away, her fingers weak from the crushing grip. The threat was clear.

"It is time to return you to your world."

Kela returned to the soft spot where she had fallen into this world. "I—I want to know . . ." she stammered. Part of her wanted to get as far away as possible, but she wondered about this sea woman and if the stories were true. "Are there others like you?"

"Yes," Ophidia replied.

Kela blinked as she lowered her body. "Where are they? Do you live with them?"

Ophidia tossed her head back, a spark of irritation flickering. "I prefer a solitary life."

"That sounds lonely."

"It is my choice and no concern of yours."

A question had been burning in Kela's thoughts since Joyce had examined the comb. She hesitated a moment, then asked, "Who is M?"

Ophidia froze and stared at Kela with a penetrating glare.

"What do you mean?"

"I saw a girl in the water. When I touched the comb," Kela whispered in fear. "She needed help. And a letter M is etched on the comb."

Ophidia studied Kela for what seemed like eons.

"Someone . . . I knew long ago," Ophidia said.

"What happened to her?"

Ophidia's eyes turned to slits and her teeth flashed. It was one question too many.

"It doesn't matter!" The sharp retort caused Kela to tumble back in the sand.

Ophidia towered defiantly. "The comb has been mine for more moons than you will ever see."

Anger swam in the current of her voice as she turned, but also something else that Kela recognized when she thought about her last words to Mum. Regret.

Ophidia swam out of sight, presumably back to her rock, and Kela sank with relief into the folds of sand. Then the singing began. Lyrical and soulful, the music exuded satisfaction.

She thought she understood why. Soon, Ophidia would have her comb back and Kela would have her wish. But that wish would come with a consequence. It wasn't clear what that meant, but she already knew what she wanted. When the time came, she wondered if she would be brave enough to wish it.

CHAPTER 13
The Wish

As she lay in bed, pieces of the night shifted like sand through Kela's brain. She remembered singing. Slowly, fragments of memory slid into place. The mirror, the water world, and the sea woman.

Pulling the covers off, she put her feet on the floor. Her toes wiggled on dry wood. The mirror on the back of her door reflected the ordinary world and pushed cool and solid against her fingers. The curtain filtered soft light through the window as she looked around her room. Clothes lay on the floor and crafts supplies cluttered her desk.

A sparkle of orange blinked from the dresser.

Ophidia's sea glass necklace peeked over the edge. Proof that everything she remembered had happened.

Her doubts about the nighttime vision vanished, but not her unease.

The final piece of her mother's rainbow.

The sea glass burned in Kela's hand. An ember she couldn't let go. She rubbed her fingers along its uneven surface, memorizing every translucent ridge and edge. When she was small, she would do this to Mum's face. Tracing her fingers over mouth and nose, cheekbones and eyes.

This necklace was once a shattered piece of glass. Sharp. Useless. Discarded. The sea transformed it. Could it rub away the shattered edges in her heart? She imagined its luminous glow throbbed an answer.

Kela's heart thumped harder as she realized what it meant. Ophidia told her to ask the sea for what she wanted. She could do that. Today.

"Time to get up!"

Flinching at Pop's sudden wake-up call, she yelled back "Coming!" She put the necklace back on the dresser and threw on a T-shirt and shorts.

Cinnamon and hot fried goodness warmed the kitchen as she sank into a chair and poured a glass of mango juice. Pop slid her a plate of crispy bakes and saltfish. Even though she had gone to bed early, her body dragged and she moved like gravity had doubled overnight.

"Sleep well?" he asked.

"Okay, I guess." She kept her eyes on her plate.

"Funny, I thought you were talking in your sleep."

"I was?" Kela put the syrup down. "I don't remember it."

"Anything you want to talk about?" Pop asked with a concerned look.

Kela circled her fork around her plate, then said, "Pop, do you believe in the seafolk?"

Pop arched his brows in surprise and laughed.

"You mean like in the stories Miss Inniss tells?"

Kela nodded.

"Well, I spend a lot of time in the water and I can't say I've ever seen even a glimpse of one. No, everyone knows they're just stories."

"Yeah," Kela agreed. Pop would never believe her about the sea woman, and she couldn't tell him what she planned to do. Just like she couldn't tell him about the comb hidden in her room. The secret pressed down on her.

"Well, eat up," Pop said with a sigh. He poured himself another cup of coffee. "I need to get to work. Are you coming?"

"No, I want to go to the beach."

"No problem. I can give you a ride."

"It's okay," Kela said. "I'll walk."

A shadow of worry crossed Pop's face, but soon his old truck rumbled away.

Kela traced her fork around the outside of her plate. Too many sides complicated the problem. Ophidia demanded that she return the comb to the sea and fulfill her end of the bargain.

That seemed simple enough, but it wasn't.

If Kela threw the comb back into the ocean today, that might cause other problems. According to Joyce, it was valuable, possibly irreplaceable. She also said she might report it to the Ministry of Culture, and that Pop could get in trouble if he hadn't yet reported it himself.

He didn't even know about it! What would happen if the comb disappeared completely? People would think he had sold it illegally.

Kela sighed and walked over to the sink to wash the dishes. Drying her hands on the old yellow dishcloth, she leaned against the counter. She knew what she had to do.

She couldn't throw the comb back yet. Not until she fixed the trouble she'd caused for Pop. But what she wanted now couldn't wait.

Within moments, Kela was trudging along the gravelly road to the beach, the heavy box in her bag bumping her side. She kicked a stone and watched it skitter a few meters ahead of her.

As she entered the market square, she focused on her wish instead. Thinking of what she wanted with all her heart, now she had to make it happen.

"You're doing it again." Lissy leaned on the counter in her grandmother's shop and waved Kela over.

"What?"

"You were about to walk by without saying hello."

"I wasn't," Kela said. Then she added, "Well, I might have been, but only because I was thinking."

"About what?"

Miss Inniss rang up purchases for Mike, a young taxi driver at the resort. Everyone called his car the "party cab" because he played soca music so loud, the air vibrated from the bass of his subwoofer when he drove by.

Kela told Lissy about the dream, or whatever it had been, about Ophidia, and the wish. Her friend listened, but Kela wasn't sure if Lissy believed her. She wasn't sure she believed it herself!

Before Lissy could respond, her grandmother walked over.

"What's going on in your head today, girl?" Miss Inniss asked. "You look worried. Everything all right?"

Kela didn't want to talk to anyone about her plan. Deep down, she knew it might be dangerous somehow, but she forced those thoughts away.

"Tired, I guess. I didn't sleep well."

"Do you want to keep us company for a while?" Miss Inniss asked. "You can help Lissy sort the postcards."

"I can't—I need to get to the beach."

Lissy gave her a questioning look but didn't say anything.

"I understand," Miss Inniss said. She added, "I'm sorry you haven't found your special glass yet."

Kela cocked her head, confused.

"When your father picked up your dinner last night, he told me you've been anxious about finding the orange sea glass you want." She hesitated. "Is that why you asked about the seafolk yesterday? Mermaids' tears?"

Kela's eyes widened, but she could only nod. Miss Inniss didn't know that the orange sea glass sat on her dresser at home.

"If I had known why you were asking, I wouldn't have gone on so much," Miss Inniss said. "You can't look into those waters and not imagine what lives down there." She put a soft hand on Kela's small one.

A customer with an armful of souvenirs came to the register, and Lissy walked over to ring her up.

Kela thought quietly, then asked Miss Inniss, "If

you were given a wish, what would you wish for?"

Miss Inniss laughed. "Me? Oh, I don't know. I think I have just about everything I need."

"But I don't mean just for things you need. What would you wish for if you could have anything?"

Miss Inniss stared out the window a long while before she responded. "I would wish for my loved ones to be happy."

"Why wouldn't you wish for yourself to be happy?" Kela asked in surprise. "If you're happy, wouldn't they be happy too?"

"No, I don't think they are the same," Miss Inniss said. "If I wish for something for myself, only I feel happy. But if I wish to make someone I love happy, then I think that would make me happy too."

Miss Inniss's words made an odd kind of sense to Kela. Now she wondered about her own wish.

Miss Inniss tipped a small bowl at Kela. "Here. Butter rums always make me happy."

Kela took a few pieces of hard yellow candy from the bowl.

"I have to go."

"Okay, dear."

Kela waved at Lissy and walked out of the shop, sucking on her piece of butter rum. Was she being selfish? Her wish would make her happy, but wouldn't it make other people happy too?

At the beach, a golden sun baked the sand. Light bounced off the surface of the water like shattered diamonds. Or mermaids' tears.

Ophidia's warning clouded her thoughts, but breathing deeply, Kela thought about what she truly wanted. She exhaled. It was worth the price.

Kela removed the box from her bag. She opened it and suddenly remembered Joyce's warning. The comb had a thin crack and it shouldn't be handled. But Ophidia said Kela should rake the comb across the water and "tell the sea" her wish.

Kela shaded her eyes and peered closely at the comb. The hairline crack was barely visible along its upper ridge. She had steady hands and had always been careful, a skill she had honed through her jewelry work. What she wanted was so close; she could feel it slipping away like the tide rushing out to sea. She closed her eyes and filled her lungs with the salt air. She could do this. It was the only way.

Lifting the comb gently out of the box, she walked into the water. Soft sand gave way to the pebbly surface of the ocean. She wobbled, off-balance, but kept moving. When she reached the point where the water swished below her shorts, she stopped.

Cradling the smooth edges of the comb, she tried to

calm the swooping in her chest. Miss Inniss's words echoed in Kela's ears and added to the sick feeling.

You don't want to get between a sea woman and her comb. Sure enough, that sea woman will come for what's hers.

As carefully as possible, she touched the tines of the comb to the salt water and swiped slowly, slicing the waves from one side to the other. She closed her eyes and wished, her heart full.

The comb broke in half.

CHAPTER 14
A Debt Unpaid

Crick.

Crack.

This is a story.

"It is done," the sea whispered.

The ancient wheel clicked forward. A wish made. A wish granted. The slow leaching of magic from Ophidia's body flexed a muscle not used in many years. She gloried in her strength, then pain ripped through her chest. She screamed in agony.

The comb was broken.

So was this how her story would end?

Against wisdom, she had once trusted a human.

The mistake awakened her to a painful truth. Betrayal.

The first had happened centuries ago, but Ophidia remembered every detail. A heavy net had entrapped her like the arms of an octopus. The night rang with her desperate cries.

The sea had intervened. A thunderous wave slammed the boat, and the net released her. The girl and the man toppled into the water. The man struggled back aboard, but the girl did not.

A friend lost.

By the time Ophidia had freed herself from the tangle of net, the life had left her friend's eyes and would not return. She caressed the girl's still face, blue in the watery light.

All Ophidia had left was the hair comb that the girl had given her, carved by her father.

Ophidia cried her first and last tear. One born of treachery and deceit. If not for the sea's help, she would have been captured. Salt bound with salt and crystallized in the waves. Bright orange it blazed, the brilliant color of the madras fabric her once-friend so loved to wear. The sharpness of that loss rankled from sadness to anger. Hanging around the sea woman's throat, the shard reminded her to never trust a human again.

And this girl, Kela?

When the waves carried her wish, the choice didn't surprise Ophidia. A shattered heart is easy to read. As expected, the girl wished for something that was impossible. Nearly.

Old magic pulsed strongest and the sea woman's years gave her great power, but the girl would pay a price for her treachery. As Ophidia was now incomplete, so also was the girl's wish. She rubbed the dulling scales of her tail; they would fall soon. Her hair would grow limp and her beautiful skin would sag from her bones.

Only a short time remained, but it was clear the girl did not intend to fulfill her promise.

Ophidia returned to the empty cavern where she last hid her soul. Fear and anger festered like a wound.

"Rest, my child," the sea said. "You will need your strength again."

Ophidia closed her eyes and let the current and her mother's voice rock her to sleep.

Crick.

Crack.

The story is put on you.

CHAPTER 15

Fragments of Glass

Her hand was empty.

Kela opened her eyes in horror and lunged at the two sinking pieces of the comb, scooping them out of the water. What had she done? She tried to push the pieces back together, but it was hopeless.

Her wish. Did a broken comb have any magic?

The sky shone as blue and welcoming as it had before. The ocean rippled around her legs. People laughed with friends as they walked along the shore. But she waited for something specific. Soft footsteps. A touch to her hair. Her name.

Nothing.

She hadn't known what to expect, but the lack of response scared her most of all. If the wish had worked, surely there would be some sign.

But the world spun on exactly the same.

Maybe it had been an awful trick. Or maybe she had ruined it all. She looked at the broken comb in her hand and was overcome with a powerful urge to hurl it far into the cresting waves.

But she couldn't. Not yet. She owed it to Pop to undo the mess she had caused. There would be time to keep her promise to Ophidia. Her neck prickled at the thought.

How would the sea woman react to her comb being broken? Kela didn't know, but she had an inkling that it wouldn't be good. She would explain that it had been an accident. Maybe she could fix the comb before she returned it to the sea.

Heart pounding, Kela tucked the two pieces back into the box and returned it to her bag.

Uneven planks thumped underfoot as she walked toward her father's shop. At Blue Water Dive, a white boat bobbed at the dock. Kela's throat tightened as she read the name. *Rose.* Her mother's name.

A whitewashed sign dangled above Kela as she opened the door. The bell jingled and a dark-skinned woman with long dreadlocks smiled from the counter.

"Storm didn't knock you over?" Shannon asked.

The shop manager tucked a thick auburn loc behind her ear.

"Nope, still here. Do you need any help?" Kela asked as she leaned against the counter.

Except for a mop and bucket in the corner, few signs of the storm remained. Swim shoes, vests, and gear hung along a wall, and air tanks leaned in cages. Neon T-shirts and visors emblazoned with Blue Water Dive's wavy logo filled the remaining space.

"Some leaks brought in water, but nothing important broke." Shannon leaned forward.

The bell rang again and two customers entered.

"I need to help these folks, so go on back," Shannon said before she turned to the young couple browsing wet suits.

Kela entered the back hall.

Loud voices punched through the walls of the office. She pressed herself flat against the corridor to listen.

"I made the call, because it was the right thing to do." Kela barely recognized Pop's angry voice. "We can't jeopardize our reputation over something like this."

"I thought we were partners? How come you didn't

tell me before you did that? Don't I have a say?"

"Of course, but I don't think it would have changed anything. I'm sorry I didn't talk to you first, but if this comb is important historically, we need to be professionals. We're a responsible diving operation, George, not treasure hunters."

Her breath caught in her throat. She hadn't been thinking. Of course Joyce would call Pop. Kela tried to be as silent as possible.

"I know we're not treasure hunters," George said, "but we need to make a living. Have you taken a look at these books?" Papers rustled and Kela pictured the stack of binders that always cluttered his desk. "We're sinking fast, man. That woman didn't call the Ministry. We could have talked to her. Finding something like this is like winning the lottery. Why would we throw that away?"

"I'm not throwing anything away."

"Then what was the rush?" George said. "Now we're stuck. Let the Ministry pay a finder's fee if they really want it. Other people might pay more though."

Pop's voice resonated clearly in the hall. "We both grew up on St. Rita. Why would we go selling off pieces of it to rich tourists?" Pop paused. "Why are you so knotted up about this? Is there something else going on here, man?"

"No!" George said, his voice creeping higher. "My father started this place, and I just don't want to see it go down. Those tourists might cough up enough for us to stay here another five or ten years. What are you going to do if we close? History won't pay the bills." George lowered his voice. "Look, you've got a daughter to look after. You have just as much, if not more, to lose than me."

"Don't go there, George," Pop said, a note of warning in his voice. "I can take care of my daughter well enough. But I am also going to teach her that there's more to life than money."

"Didn't mean anything by it," George backpedaled. "I just want us to think through all the options."

"Yeah, I get it. Regardless of whether we agree or disagree, it's done now. I've called the Ministry of Culture. An officer will be contacting us to complete a report."

"I need some air," George said.

Kela realized too late that footsteps were approaching the office door. George didn't see her at first. A frown marred his usually jovial face, but when he saw her standing in the hallway, he put on his familiar grin.

"Kela—you've been keeping a secret."

Pop came to the door and there was no escape.

"We need to talk," he said sternly.

"I've got a lesson at the resort," George said. He tugged lightly on one of Kela's braids and then walked out the back door.

Kela smoothed her hair and entered the door Pop was holding open for her. After she sat down, he started.

"How could you find something like that and not tell me?"

"I'm sorry, Pop. I didn't know what it was when I found it."

"But you know that you should have shown it to me," he said, the muscles in his jaw clenched tight. "Joyce called me and told me what you showed her. Do you know how it felt to hear about this from her? She said you found it during a dive. I haven't been able to get you to dive since—" He stopped. "You should have told me."

"I wanted to," Kela said. She slid her sandal back and forth. It scratched and scraped against the linoleum. "I was afraid of what you'd say."

"I thought we agreed last night that we weren't going to keep any more secrets from each other," he said quietly.

She could only gulp down the guilt in her throat.

"So where did you find it?"

"Coral Gardens Cave."

Pop sat down and rubbed his hand over his head. "You're telling me you took that box from a protected reserve?"

Kela nodded. The tension in the tiny room crackled.

Pop shook his head. "I have no words." He rubbed his head again. "Well, it's done. Let me take a look so I know what has caused all this commotion."

Opening her bag, she slowly took the box out and gave it to Pop.

"Joyce didn't mention it being in pieces," Pop said with a frown.

"I know," Kela said. "It was an accident."

Pop closed his eyes and the room filled with angry silence. "Well," he said finally after an agonizing wait, "I can see what Joyce was going on about. You never should have taken this."

"I'm sorry. What's going to happen now?"

"We try to avoid jail," Pop said with a wry smile as Kela's eyes widened. He waved his hand for her to calm. "We face fines, but if we are cooperative, we might avoid those and any serious legal troubles. Hopefully, the right professionals can restore this."

Pop closed the box gently. Kela reached her hand out, but Pop turned his back to her.

"I'm locking it up. I'm accountable for it now."

Pop crossed the room to the gray wall safe, entered the combination, and put the box inside. She clenched her palms and tried to keep hope, but inside a hollow echoed.

The *click* of the lock sounded like a cannon in her ears.

She had no choice but to go. Pop went back to work, frustration still thick in the room.

"I'm disappointed in you," he said.

Kela flinched. Those words stung worse than anything.

The worn linoleum flooring creaked as Kela walked down the hallway to the storage room. Diving equipment and boat parts littered the space, and the air smelled of salt and motor oil. A plastic tub sat near the service door along with a folding table and chair, and a chalked sign leaned against the wall.

Kela's Kreations
JEWELRY FROM THE SEA

Dropping her bag, she dug in the plastic container, removed a jar of sea glass in all shapes and sizes, and took it to the workbench. The fragments poured out as she turned the jar, and she studied them. A puzzle in glass.

With the comb locked up, she had no way to return the comb to Ophidia. Kela's stomach flip-flopped and she tapped her feet as she tried to think of options.

Forcing herself to routines, Kela dropped the sea glass into another jar containing a vinegar solution she used for cleaning. Screwing the lid back on the jar, she twisted her wrist and swirled a tiny tornado of sand and grit.

The bell over the front door jingled faintly, signaling that Shannon had more customers.

Kela rolled the jar in her hands, looking for inspiration and answers. Even jewelry pieces she planned might end up looking completely different once she started. The sea told the story and she wrote it with fingers and cord.

Footsteps approached.

"One of my meetings was rescheduled, so I have the afternoon free. Do you want to run some errands with me?"

Kela turned and the jar of sea glass tumbled from her fingers. It hit the floor, sending fragments and liquid everywhere, but she didn't care. In the doorway was the person she wanted to see most.

Her mother was back.

CHAPTER 16
The Key

Crick.

Crack.

This is a story.

Through fate's twists and turns, Ophidia had parlayed with humans for centuries. One truth had guided her.

Human intentions did not ensure they would keep their promises.

This girl, Kela. Her greatest desire was to be with her mother. Ophidia's brow furrowed in bitterness. Love. She had been betrayed for as much before.

Ophidia would not wait idly for death. The girl would sleep for eternity in the bottom of the waves. Ophidia would use her last breath to make it so.

How would the sea woman exact this revenge?

Much lay hidden in the deep. Where no eyes could see, where no breath could be taken, horrors lay in wait. Brooding in the dark. Hungering for release. One only needed the key.

But it had been lost.

Then the girl showed her the way—although she didn't know it. They were connected. Ophidia sensed the key in a place filled with dust and memories. She scoffed at the human need to record their past to remember. The sea remembered all.

Humans had set the key among other stolen treasures. To retrieve it, Ophidia would have to walk among them. The idea disgusted her. However, it was a price she would pay. Exchanging her beauty for their clumsy, misshapen legs, the sea woman would take back what belonged in the deep.

With single-minded venom, she wound along the black currents toward the island.

Crick.

Crack.

The story is put on you.

CHAPTER 17

Wish Fulfilled

Afraid she would blink away the woman standing before her, Kela stood frozen. Thick lashes and deep brown eyes looked back at her from a troubled face. Emotions she forgot she had bubbled inside and pressed hard against her chest. As her brain worked to understand, Kela realized she was holding her breath.

"Are you okay?" Mum said.

Then the force holding Kela in place dissolved. Wrapping her arms fiercely around Mum, she buried her head in the soft warmth of her flesh-and-blood reality. She wanted to crawl into her mother's arms and live there forever. In the distance, a soft and fragile cry wavered. Kela realized it was coming from her.

Mum staggered from the force of Kela's hug but returned the embrace. She laid her head on top of Kela's and swayed.

"Shhh . . ." Mum said. "It's all right. Honey, what's wrong?"

"I can't believe you're here." She struggled to put her feelings into words. "I love you and I didn't mean what I said before. I don't hate you. I love you and I missed you so much."

"What? Kela! What are you talking about?"

"I'm sorry I said I hate you."

"Oh honey, you're still thinking about that?" her mother said with a gentle squeeze. "That was months ago. I know that you don't hate me, but I knew that already. We all get angry and say things we don't mean." She stroked Kela's braids. "Is something else wrong?"

Everything was upside down. Months ago? She had believed she would never see her mother again and now here Mum stood. She willed her legs to hold her up as she tried to compose herself.

"I'm fine, Mum. I just dropped my jar."

"Well, I think we ought to clean up this mess before someone gets cut. Will you look in the corner and see if you can find the broom?"

Kela held on a moment more, then let go. Her

eyes tracked her mother, afraid to release her. Mum carefully began picking up the biggest fragments of glass. Finding the broom and dustpan, Kela walked back to her.

"Here, I'll sweep," Mum said.

While Mum swept all the pieces to the center of the room, Kela pulled another jar out of her tub and gingerly picked out the pieces of sea glass that were salvageable. Her mother swept the rest into the dustpan and emptied it into the trash.

"So, what were you planning to make?" she asked.

"A necklace," Kela said. "Miss Inniss sold everything I brought her last week."

"Oh, that's too bad. I'm sure it would have been lovely. Hopefully some of the glass is still usable. Maybe we should take another trip to the beach? We haven't done any searching together in a while."

"Great," Kela said croakily. "I've missed spending time with you."

"Me too," her mother said, cupping Kela's face in her hands.

Mum walked toward the door. "Come on. Let's go tell Pop you're leaving with me."

Kela wondered what would happen when Pop saw her. Mum was here acting like the accident never happened. Grabbing her bag, she followed Mum to the office. Her mother knocked once on the door and entered.

Pop sat at his desk, a frown on his face. As soon as they walked in the door, he brightened.

"My other favorite girl!" He walked over and gave his wife a short kiss. "Did you just get here?"

Kela leaned against the door for support. Whatever magic Ophidia had, it had done its job well. Pop didn't look like a man whose dead wife had just walked into the room. He was himself, the way he was before the accident, and he did not seem the least bit afraid that he might be talking to a ghost.

"Yes, we're going to run some errands, then meet you at home, okay?"

"Fine. Things are sort of hectic here and it's not a good time for me to leave," Pop said.

"What's going on?" Mum asked.

"I just found out Kela took something from the coral reserve the other day," he said with a stern glance toward Kela. "Take a look."

He took the small box out of the safe and opened it.

"What a shame it's broken, but how lovely!" She turned to Kela, mirroring Pop's serious expression. "What would possess you to collect from the reserve? We've taught you better."

Kela ducked her head, but she didn't care. Mum's

scolding was better than all the months of silence she had endured.

Her father put the box back in the safe and locked it again. "George and I are having some disagreements, though." Pop sat down with a heavy sigh.

"About what?" Mum asked.

"He's more than a little upset that I've already reported it to the Ministry of Culture. He thinks we could sell it. Even broken, it's valuable."

"You're not going to do that, are you?"

"Of course not," Pop said with a sigh. "We'll talk it out later." He held the door open. "Why don't you go and do what you need to. We can talk more at dinner."

"Okay," Mum said. "Be home on time. I'm cooking fish cakes tonight."

"I'll make sure I am."

Kela and Mum walked to the storage room and out the back door. She couldn't believe she was going to spend an afternoon with her mother running errands. Three months ago, she would have dreaded this, but today was not three months ago.

Until she could get the comb, she wouldn't waste one minute away from Mum.

In Kela's chest, her heart switched places with the sun. Warmth pounded inside her and threatened to shoot out as she walked next to her very real mother. Not a copy or a fake, but a real person who dug in her purse for candy and handed Kela the piece with the least lint sticking to the wrapper. Kela unwrapped the honey-colored butter rum and let the sweetness flood her mouth.

"So what do we need to do today?" she asked.

"The clasp on my bracelet is broken." Mum pulled the sparkling chain from her purse. Kela knew it well. She had picked it out. Gold with three dazzling birthstones. Amethyst for Mum, aquamarine for Pop, and topaz for herself. The last place she had seen it was in her mother's casket.

"So we need to run by the jewelry shop." Mum pulled her car keys out of her purse. "Is there anything you need for your crafting?"

Kela thought about what she wanted to make for Miss Inniss's shop. "I could use some more crochet thread, since I'm almost out of blue. That color sells faster."

"I think your pieces are beautiful," Mum said. "I can't imagine what you'll be making when you are older. That reminds me. You haven't touched the application packet yet for the Caribbean Youth Creative Arts Program. You promised me you'd go."

Kela had. The program was hosted annually

in St. Vincent. Even more than having her work displayed around the island and being considered an artist, she dreamed of traveling beyond St. Rita someday. Mum's death had made her stop thinking about that, but hope and possibility now walked and talked beside her.

"Sometimes . . ." Kela searched for the words to capture her longing. "I think about making things that could be seen all over the world, not just in St. Rita. I'd love to bring the feeling of the ocean to more people."

"And you can." Mum squeezed her as they walked to the car. "You have so much to share and you will make that happen."

Hastings Fine Jewelry had broad windows and vivid blue double doors. As Kela and Mum entered, they saw brightly lit glass cabinets that snaked along the outside walls. Tourists browsed displays in the center of the room. A store associate helped a couple paying for a purchase. Another man talked to an employee at the far end. His back was to Kela, but he seemed familiar. The two men disappeared through a door marked "Private."

A sales associate approached them. "Can I show you something today?"

"My husband bought me a bracelet here a few

months ago. The clasp is loose and I need it repaired." Kela's mother handed her bracelet to the woman.

"Yes, of course. I'll start the paperwork and get you on your way."

When the form was finished, the associate took the bracelet back to the repair shop. As they waited, Kela saw the door marked "Private" open. When the men came out, she recognized George.

He shook the other man's hand and walked toward the front door. His eyes widened as he recognized Kela and Mum.

"Hi," Kela said.

Mum looked up in surprise. "George! How are you?"

"Hello, ladies."

George's smile seemed pasted on. He clearly hadn't expected to see them. Yet he wasn't surprised that Mum was alive. Like Pop, he accepted Mum's reappearance without question.

"What are you doing here? Buying something for yourself or a lady friend?" Mum asked with amusement.

"Oh . . . something for myself. I was thinking about a new watch."

"Why were you back there?" Kela pointed toward the back.

Mum glanced at the door marked "Private."

"Kela, don't be rude."

George looked uncomfortable. "I—don't like shopping. I wanted to see some things in private." His smile stretched as an awkward silence lingered. "I've got to run," he said at last. "I'll catch you both later!" He slid past them and walked briskly from the shop.

Kela's mother shrugged and turned to the clerk who had just returned, but Kela stared after George. If the business was struggling like her father had said, what was George doing here?

CHAPTER 18
The Sea Hag

Crick.
Crack.
This is a story.

The sea woman called to the sea, "Give me legs."

The current brought a gift from her mother, or rather a curse. In the sunless tide, a scarf as red as blood billowed. Ophidia tied it around her tangled mane. She wanted no part of the human world, but her purpose outweighed her revulsion.

With the final knot tied, pain like she had never felt stabbed through her.

Slicing. Ripping. Mutilating. No one but the sea

heard her screams.

She staggered from the waves into a quiet cove. Trading her tail stripped Ophidia of the glamour of immortality. No longer thwarted by the sea, time reveled in her unmasking.

Weak and trembling, Ophidia wobbled on the two wrinkled stubs that had replaced her tail of green and gold. Her hands had sloughed off their youth and were now withered and spotted with age. A plain shift and shawl as gray as the stormy sea hung on her skeletal frame. She tottered forward and grimaced. Coverings made of dried animal skins encased her feet, covering their hideousness.

Sparse white hair lay tangled and matted against her head, bound still in the crimson scarf.

"Mother, do you need help?" a tiny voice said.

Ophidia snapped her head in the direction of the child who spoke, and he stopped. His eyes widened with fear.

"Where is the road?" she rasped.

The boy pointed to a path that led from the beach. When she moved away from the surf, he ran.

Each step jabbed like knives into the bottoms of her feet. The heat of the sun baked her thin brown skin. The pain fueled her rage.

At the entrance to a building, she labored up each

step. People backed out of her path, held doors open, refused to look her in the eyes. Magic still pulsed around her, but so did fear.

In the museum, she only had to look at a person and they silently pointed in the direction she sought. No one stopped her. Her body creaked as she moved.

Her clouded eyes squinted in the fluorescence of the final room. She approached the exhibit. The sign read "Natural History Wing: Prehistoric Fossils."

The bones of ancient creatures great and small lay littered in a case of glass and wood. Her eyes focused on the largest. Glistening black and triangular. Its edges jagged and made for cutting. She glanced at the label. "*Carcharocles megalodon*. Cenozoic Era." She smiled.

The human name, megalodon, came from one of their ancient languages. It meant "large tooth." They were right. And wrong. It was a tooth, but not from any creature long dead.

It was the key that would release something very much alive.

Ophidia placed her hand on the glass, and it dissolved into fine crystals. Glass was but sand and salt. She lifted the key and hobbled from the room.

She had what she sought. Now, step by torturous step, she walked back toward the sea. In the blazing orange of the setting sun, a final task settled in her mind.

A message the girl would not miss.

Crick.
Crack.
The story is put on you.

CHAPTER 19
Slinking Shadows

Savory aromas wrapped the kitchen in familiar warmth. A pot of rich cou cou, boiled cornmeal and okra, bubbled next to a pan steaming with seasoned fish. Spicy fish cakes hissed in fry oil.

Kela had been lingering in the kitchen much longer than normal and her mother had finally noticed.

"I've got dinner under control," Mum said.

"Are you sure you don't want me to mix up the mauby?" Kela asked.

"No, you already put the groceries away and set the table. You look tired. Go on now. You can help me wash up later." Mum's smile was as broad as Kela remembered, and she couldn't help smiling too as she walked to her room.

But worry slunk along the edges of Kela's now perfect life. Although she pushed it away, the nagging was like an insistent itch. She had promised to return the comb. Thinking about the problem was well and good, but it didn't bring her closer to a solution.

She hadn't really believed in magic combs and wishes. But her proof now stood in the kitchen cooking dinner and humming her favorite Carnival song. Pulling out a piece of sea glass Mum found on the beach, Kela turned it in her hand. Now that she had what she wanted most, and knew it was real, she saw how this new life could be taken away in an instant. Disquiet fluttered like butterflies in her chest.

Kela remembered the orange sea glass necklace. She couldn't believe she had forgotten it! She had to show Mum that she had completed their rainbow. Excitement drained as her eyes settled on the dresser.

The necklace was gone.

An uneasy chill inched up Kela's spine. Puzzled, she walked over to her dresser and checked behind her jewelry box and moved her hair ties. On the floor and even under the furniture, she pawed through forgotten odds and ends and dust balls that had set up home. It wasn't there.

The mirror on the back of her door still pressed solidly against her fingers, nothing like the shimmery surface of the night before. Shaking the thoughts from her brain, she opened the door and went back to the kitchen.

Pop came home as Mum took the last of the fish cakes out of the frying pan. He leaned back against the sink and drank a cool ginger beer. His gear bag sat by his feet.

Kela saw a chance, hoping that perhaps her father had brought the comb home to put in the bedroom safe. He had said he was responsible for it now, and if she could get it out of the box before he locked it up, she could return it to Ophidia. She didn't care about the Ministry anymore. Mum was more important than that.

She bounced over to Pop and picked up his bag. "I can put this in your room. Dinner's almost ready."

"Now *that's* service," he said. "I'm going to get spoiled from all this special attention. A nice meal and a valet!"

Grinning, Kela hauled the bag down the hall to her parents' room. Inside, she closed the door and unzipped the bag slowly so it wouldn't make a sound.

Goggles, a waterproof camera, an underwater

flashlight, and several other items tumbled as her fingers rummaged deeper into the bag. Frustration grew and she huffed. The box wasn't there.

She re-zipped the bag roughly and panic rose inside her, but she pushed it back down and took a deep breath. After she calmed, she walked slowly to the kitchen. Pop was already eating with relish and Mum handed her a plate.

"So, did you two have a good day?" Pop dipped a fish cake into sauce.

"Yeah." Kela sat down at the table, trying to keep her voice from wavering. "Mum and I went to the craft store and the beach."

"We also went to the jewelers to get my bracelet fixed," said Mum. "Hendy, do you know if George has a lady friend?"

Pop swallowed thickly and looked up with a wry smile. "Why do you ask that?" he said, taking another swig of ginger beer.

"We saw him at the jewelry shop," Kela said. "Mum asked him if he was buying for himself or someone special." She smirked at the last word.

"Well, if he does, it's not someone he's mentioned to me. That's funny though. He's usually so tight with money."

The oddly normal dinner amazed Kela. Her father talked about the diving lessons he'd given to a couple on their honeymoon. Mum vented about funding problems for her current research project. She seemed to spend as much time chasing funding as she did documenting the island's folklore.

It was everything Kela had missed. A warmth swelled inside her when she realized her wish had come true. They were a family again.

"Are you all right?" Mum asked, noticing Kela's smile.

"I'm happy we're all home," she said.

"I am too," Mum said, resting her hand on Kela's arm.

After dinner, Kela approached her bedroom and briny air prickled her nose. She opened her door and could see that the floor was dry, but despite that, her heart thumped loudly. She stepped in and closed the door.

Her mirror hung on the back, but the reflection was not her own. Kela tried to stifle the scream clawing up her throat. Dark locs and two golden snake eyes. Silver and green glinted with brown as Ophidia's face glared through the shimmery surface. She gripped the orange shard of sea glass in her long, sharp fingers.

Her mouth shaped a word Kela could not hear, but she understood. As the image faded, the word was branded in her memory.

Soon.

She was running out of time.

CHAPTER 20

Promises to Break

"Why is your mirror out there?" Pop said.

Kela sat at the table finishing her morning bowl of hot cereal, and Pop had noticed the broken mirror in the trash outside.

"I shut my door too hard last night and it fell," she said. "Sorry."

Ophidia's silent warning filed her nerves raw, and she had not slept. Ophidia had promised to drag Kela to the bottom of the waves if the comb wasn't returned. The threat was real.

After the terrifying image had faded, Kela had taken down the mirror and wrapped it in a blanket. Careful not to wake her parents, she carried it to the backyard and stepped all over its surface, shattering it to useless bits. She wished she could break every mirror in the house. She didn't need any more reminders.

Passing through the mirror had been magical, but now she saw it for what it was. An open door. If she could go in, what stopped something else from coming out?

"You should have called one of us for help," Mum said. She had just entered the kitchen, but apparently she had been listening from the other room.

"I know."

Mum rummaged in her work bag and opened and closed drawers more than once. "I need to go," she said absently.

"Are you okay?"

"I'm not sure where my head is this morning." Mum rubbed her temple and leaned against the counter. "I don't feel like I got any sleep." She gave up on what she had been hunting for and picked up her bag.

"Take it easy, honey," Pop said.

"I will." She kissed him and then Kela on the head before leaving.

"I'm going too. Coming?" Pop said to Kela.

"Okay. I need my other supplies from the shop." The comb was still locked in the safe and she wanted to stay close and be ready for a chance to take it back.

"We've got to hurry since I told Shannon that I would open up," Pop said.

Kela grabbed her bag and followed her father.

Down the curving road into Baytown, people waved from their porches. The sky radiated an endless blue dotted with clouds. Kela couldn't wait to tell Lissy what had happened. Mum was back and everything they had learned about the seafolk was true!

Within minutes, she and Pop passed the resort and parked the truck near the dock.

At the end of the pier, Pop pulled out his keys. "Wait," he said.

The front door of the shop stood ajar. He listened, then pushed open the door.

The shop had been ransacked. Inside the store, racks of clothes were knocked over, accessories pulled down from their displays, and glass cabinets smashed.

Pop entered the store and gaped at the destroyed merchandise and empty shelves. Kela peeked from behind him and saw that the door leading to the business office was hanging off its hinges. Pop turned, pushed her back out, then made a call on his cell phone.

"I'd like to report a break-in." Tension rimmed his voice. "Yes, I'm here now. I own Blue Water Dive and just arrived to unlock the building, but the door was open."

He turned away, but Kela could hear his anger.

"Okay, we'll wait out front. Thanks." Pop turned back toward Kela and exhaled. "Well, someone has made a real mess in there. I won't know how bad it is until we can document what's missing."

The police arrived and disappeared from view for several minutes. "Clear!" An officer opened the door for them to enter.

One of the constables, a tall man with close-cropped hair, came over. "Can you tell us what you first noticed when you arrived?"

"As I went to put in the key, I saw that the door was already open, so I pushed it. The broken cases and merchandise everywhere stood out right away."

The constable took notes. "We'll need to get an inventory, but what items do you think are missing in the primary part of the store?"

"I don't know." Pop scanned the area. "There seem to be fewer pairs of scuba shoes. Some of the smaller items could be gone too." He glanced around the room again and then back to the officer. "Is there any way we can see the office? The things back there are much more valuable and affect our day-to-day running."

"I have a few more questions for you, but we can discuss them in the back."

They walked through the shop to the door that led to the back hallway. Broken glass and dive gear mingled everywhere. At the door, the officer stopped to let Pop and Kela enter the small room.

"We got cleaned out," Pop said through clenched teeth. "This is a nightmare."

"Start by telling me what is missing."

"Well, a computer, a printer, fax machine . . ." Pop walked over to the wall safe, which was also open, and inspected it. "And pretty much everything that was in the safe."

"Wait, the safe is empty?" Kela's heart tripped.

"The only thing left are some papers. The money and other valuables are gone."

"But Pop, what about the comb? Didn't you lock that in the safe?"

"What comb?" interrupted the constable, looking up from his notes.

"It was an antique carved bone comb. My daughter found it recently and I locked it in the safe. A lot of good that did us."

"Pop . . ." Kela remembered her hand as Lissy had tried to pull her from the sinkhole. She imagined her mother's fingers slipping through her grip instead.

Her father looked at her, and her stomach sank like frozen mud. How could she return the comb to

Ophidia if it had been stolen?

"It'll be okay," her father said, trying to reassure her. He turned to the officer. "What do you think the chances are of recovering it? It's very unique."

"We'll notify the local galleries," the officer said. "If someone tries to unload it through the mainstream channels, we'll catch them. If the thief is smart, they won't try that and will hold on to it. If they don't sell it, we might have to wait quite a while until it resurfaces."

"I just can't believe this has happened. We've been at this location for years and nothing like this has happened before."

Another officer came in and said something to the first.

"Mr. Boxhill, who else has a key to the building?"

"Just my partner, George Arthur, and our store manager, Shannon Greene. George should be arriving soon. A dive is scheduled for later this morning. Shannon should be here any moment too. She had a doctor's appointment and asked if I could open the shop today."

"And do you know the last time either of them was on the premises?"

"Yes. George left around one or two p.m. yesterday and Shannon left right before I did at about five. The place was shut up tight."

"We're going to have to talk to them," the officer said.

Kela followed Pop to the front, her numb body moving automatically. The front door opened and George stared in shock.

"What's going on here?"

"We've been robbed, George," Pop said gruffly.

"What! How did they get in?" George glanced all around the shop.

"We're trying to put together a timeline of who was here and when," said the constable who had talked to Pop. "You can help us, Mr. Arthur. Can you tell me when you left the shop?"

"I left earlier in the afternoon," George said somewhat quickly. "Hendy said he would close up."

"Pop," Kela interrupted, "I'm going back up to the beach."

"That's fine," he said with half a glance in her direction.

She grabbed her supplies from the storage room and left out the back.

Dread weighed on her as she walked up the pier. How could she return a comb she didn't have? She couldn't. Ophidia would come, and she wouldn't let a broken mirror stop her.

CHAPTER 21

Sea Heart

Heat radiated from the sand as Kela picked her way across the beach. At the base of her favorite palm tree, she collapsed and closed her eyes, her head cradled in the sway of the trunk. A line of sweat marched down her back like a column of ants.

Trying to slow her breathing and organize her thoughts was impossible. Her mother's life was in the hands of whatever thief had stolen the comb. She kicked the sand as sour panic filled her mouth.

Kela thought about going to see Lissy. She had been excited this morning to tell her about Mum, but that feeling had shriveled to dust. Lissy might react like Pop, like Mum had never died. She wouldn't understand.

Kela looked down at her bag and noticed the crinkled corner of one of the sheets she had taken from Mum's files at the historical society. She pulled out the loose pile of papers.

On top sat the letter Lissy had found. The account of the deadly hurricane of 1667 from a man named William to his sister. She read it again, then leafed through the other pages. Most were handwritten in Mum's careful script. She pulled one out.

April 2004—Interview with Mrs. Montrose Banks. Cane Hall, St. Rita. Mrs. Banks, age 102, is my maternal great-grandmother. I met with her to record a family story about an ancestor who drowned at sea. She tells me the story was passed down to her as a child by her grandmother Mrs. Etheline Motts.

Kela never knew that Mum had officially recorded the stories from her family. Even in the heat of the late morning sun, a chill raised the hairs on Kela's neck.

Quashey was a free colored man. He was known around the island for his fine carving skill. His greatest wish was to buy his wife's freedom as he had for his two children, Meera and Occo. One evening, he heard Meera singing a strange tune as she put her sister to bed.

He asked her where she had learned it and she said from her "water friend." He knew she had met one of the seafolk. He asked her to take him to hear the song too, and since she loved her papa, she did.

From their skiff, Meera called out to her "water friend." The sea woman swam up next to their boat. Her long, twisted hair floated on the waves. Meera's papa threw a net over the sea woman and caught her. "This sea woman will bring us enough money to buy your mama's freedom," he told his daughter. Meera cried and told her papa no, but he wouldn't listen.

Without warning, a powerful wave knocked them out of their boat and Meera sank beneath the water. The clouds turned black and a fierce storm whipped up. Though her papa got back into the boat and made it to shore, he never saw his older daughter again; all he had was little Occo. "And the sea raged. My grannie said everyone on the island felt its anger that night," said Mrs. Banks.

Kela let the page rest in her lap.

There was a letter *M* etched on the back of the comb. Could the girl in her vision be this Meera? She read the story again. A sea woman. A storm. So many similarities and so many questions.

The date of the storm in the letter, 1667, was over three hundred and fifty years ago. Could the sea woman in the story be Ophidia?

Kela restacked the papers and shoved them back in her bag. She pulled herself up and brushed off her sand-crusted shorts. She knew she should be excited by this discovery, but it only scared her more. The comb was missing and without it, she could lose her mother again.

She was Mum's only hope.

Her best thinking came when her hands were busy, so she walked back to the house. She dropped her bag in her room and pulled out her jewelry supplies. At the kitchen table, Kela took out the sea glass she had brought from the storage room and poured the pieces on the table. Sorting by size and color, she made piles: small and large, blues and greens, round and elongated.

Sea beans were pushed into their own pile. Those would look pretty strung onto a bracelet. Seeds from tropical rain forests, they had drifted for miles.

Pounded by the ocean, they made beautiful beads when polished, but if you cracked the seed coat and planted one, a germ of life might still be strong enough to sprout.

She didn't feel like making a bracelet now. Maybe a necklace? Kela had found a sea heart after the storm, a flat brown seed resembling a heart. Mum told her that in the old days, women gave sea hearts to their husbands before they sailed. They were supposed to be lucky and ensure a loved one's safe voyage.

As she held the little seed, it was like she held her own tiny heart in her hand. She had missed Mum so much, and just when everything seemed fixed, she could lose her again. Think, she told herself.

She pulled out a few sheets of fine sandpaper and began to polish the sea heart.

The robbery seemed too coincidental. The constable said the police would monitor pawn shops for unusual sales, but the thief might not use a pawn shop to get rid of the comb. As her hands rubbed a circle around the sea heart, she thought about where else a person might sell something as unique as the comb.

She considered the bits and pieces of sea glass, thread, and wire on the table. People wanted trinkets to remind them of the ocean and their trip to St. Rita.

That's one of the reasons her pieces were so popular. Tourists often visited the island's jewelry shops too. Taking something as beautiful as the comb and reducing it to a souvenir was a crime, but it might be a smart way to get it off the island.

Kela stopped sanding.

She knew who it was. Would Pop believe her? She could hardly believe it herself. Kela felt the same rising panic. There was only one way she would keep her mother.

She needed to steal the comb back.

CHAPTER 22

Slipping Away

When Mum came home that evening, the expression on her face was one Kela had never seen. She was like a person lost in a deep fog.

"What's wrong?"

Mum sank into a chair and rubbed her fingers across the well-worn wood of the kitchen table. New fears sparked in Kela.

"The little energy I woke with this morning feels gone, drained out. I can't focus on anything. I kept reading the same lines over and over and even missed an important meeting I'd worked for weeks to schedule."

"Can I do anything to help?" Kela wrapped her arms around Mum's shoulders.

"No, sweetheart," Mum said, her sigh making Kela's heart ache. "Tell Pop there are leftovers you can heat up for dinner."

As Mum shut her bedroom door, Kela frowned. Had Ophidia's magic gone wrong? Something wasn't right, but she shook her head. The magic had brought Mum back. So, she was tired. She'd feel better with some rest.

Kela sorted the beads and sea glass she had grouped into zipper bags. The rough outer shell of the sea heart she had sanded was now buffed to a natural shine, and she put it with the other beads.

Pop's truck pulled up, but two doors slammed instead of one. Miss Inniss came in with a cast-iron pot and set it on the stove. Pop carried more food.

"Is that dinner?" Kela asked. The earthy scent of bay leaves rose from the pot.

"You folks too skinny round here," Miss Inniss said, "so I fixed oxtail stew."

"Where's Lissy?" Kela said, craning her head out the door.

"She's at choir practice tonight."

The commotion in the kitchen brought Mum.

"Evelyn! I forgot you were bringing dinner."

"It's no trouble. I like to cook and you like to eat."

Kela set the table and they sat down. Mum didn't

eat much and mostly moved the food around on her plate. Kela relaxed when Mum joined in the conversation, and she wondered if she had been overreacting.

"Did the police find anything, Pop?"

Miss Inniss shook her head. "Henderson, I still can't believe someone robbed your shop. Some bodies always want something for nothing."

"Oh no!" Mum said, rousing at Miss Inniss's words. "I hadn't heard, Hendy. Why didn't you call me?"

"It's all right. I didn't want to worry you." He stabbed at his food. "At least there were no other reported break-ins on the pier."

"Do the police think the comb had anything to do with it?" Kela said.

"They find it suspicious that it was stolen the day after we reported it," Pop said. "The police talked to George and Shannon, but none of us have any ideas."

"Pop," Kela said. "What if one of them was involved?"

"That's a shocking thing to suggest," Mum said with a frown.

"How can you say that?" Pop said.

"The comb is worth a lot of money."

Pop shook his head. "I don't think Shannon would ever—"

Kela took a deep breath. "I think George stole the comb."

"What?" Pop put his fork down and stared hard at her.

"He wanted you to sell the comb and he was talking with a man at the jewelry shop," Kela said with defiance. "It had to be about the comb."

"Had to be?" Pop said with a huff. "That's a big assumption. This isn't a television detective show, and I can't believe you'd say something like that."

"Well," said Miss Inniss, putting her hand on top of Pop's clenched fist, "whoever is behind this ought to be ashamed of themselves. The police will find them out."

Pop sighed. "You're right."

Kela washed the dishes with Miss Inniss so Mum could lie down again. The sky grayed and thunder rumbled and growled.

"Another storm," said Pop, peering through the window. He shook his head in disbelief. "Evelyn, I should run you home."

"Thank you," Miss Inniss said. They gathered her dishes to carry out to the truck, and she gave Kela a quick kiss on the cheek before she bustled after Pop.

As soon as they left, the rain began. First with large scattered drops, then it shifted to a rolling downpour that made the air inside damp. Kela finished cleaning the kitchen and soon headlights blazed in the driveway again.

When her father got back inside, he was soaked from his run up the walk. After changing into some dry clothes, he sat on the couch to watch television. She wasn't very interested in the cricket match, though, and excused herself for bed.

The empty hook on the back of the door was a relief. No mirror, no way into her room. Getting rid of it wasn't likely to keep Ophidia away for good, but it made Kela feel more secure.

As she drifted to sleep, options rose and fell on waves of hope. Tomorrow might be her only chance to keep her mother.

CHAPTER 23

Up from the Sea

Crick.

Crack.

This is a story.

The storm that boiled within Ophidia rolled into
the sea. Rain slapped the land in frustration. Her
tail thrashed, and she tried not to think about her
fading life.

Seafolk didn't carry their souls like common
belongings nor cram them between flesh and bone.
They were too precious for that.

Carved from the bones of a creature long dead, the
comb—her soul cage—had been a gift of friendship.
One that proved false. Magic allowed her to trap the

soul she had taken inside. Like all seafolk, she had hidden hers, and in dark and slow-moving places, she had kept it for centuries. And she had survived.

Would a child be her downfall?

Humans had become bolder in their trespasses. Once content to stay only where their grotesque feet could go, now they dared farther. Sails sped them across the waves, and even the bottom of the sea was not safe.

The time had come for her to do more. Ophidia had taken back the necklace. The sea glass hung once again from her neck. Fear had prompted the girl to close the mirror portal. Shattered fragments were all that were left. She would deliver her next threat in person.

Traveling to the surface was not something the sea woman did without reason. Although she could breathe their bitter air, it grated in her lungs and had none of the sweetness of the sea.

The red scarf had dissolved back into the waves after her last sojourn on land. She did not need it. In her rage, she would rise in her natural glory.

Unlike moving in the water, the heaviness above the surface was burdensome. In the waves, she was graceful and free, a creature of dreams and fancy.

Humans thought her beautiful if they chanced upon her splashing in the moonlight, but they would never think so now.

Up from the depths, she broke the surface near a sandy shore. Her eyes just above the waterline, she searched. Lights twinkled from a tall building. The girl was not there. The right place lay high on the hill. Ophidia swam to a secluded cove, the storm feeding her strength.

Digging into the earth, she dragged her body out of the surf. First sand and stone, then mud and bush. Twisted hair hung limp and tangled around her dirt-streaked face, and her long fingers tore at the ground. Scales became ragged and dull as they scraped.

She didn't care.

Instead, she clawed and dragged. A whiplike flick of her tail propelled her forward while she pulled with her full might. The pouring rain made the hard earth slick, and mud formed channels beneath her weight.

Lumbering through the shadows, she inched closer. Once, a car flashed past, blinding her, and she hissed and flattened herself to the ground.

At last, the place stood before her, a small white

house nestled off the road. Tall grass covered the narrow yard, and she clenched her teeth as she thought of the girl resting inside. One who deserved no comfort tonight.

Ophidia dragged herself across the road to the grass. Fist by fist, she pulled herself closer, cocking her head left and then right, instinct and senses guiding her. There was no light, but she did not need it. Heat and movement caused her eyes to dart to the nearest window. Mud sucked at her body as she moved through the pouring rain.

At the window, she grappled the frame and lifted her face toward the glass. Two forms sat close, one with its face in its hands and the other helplessly stroking the head of the first. The remnants of magic were strong, but this was not the room she wanted. Only what she had given, magic whose price had not yet been paid, was here. Deep and low, she hissed and moved on.

Ophidia lowered herself and moved to the side of the house. As she slid to the next window, the girl's scent confirmed this was the right room. She forced herself up, splintering fragments of wood.

The girl lay asleep, untroubled by her unfulfilled promise. The sea woman gouged the windowsill with her nails. Death was coming for Ophidia, and already its salty breath peeled the skin on her neck. The girl had one more day, then, child or not, Ophidia would teach her the cost of betrayal.

Crick.
Crack.
The story is put on you.

CHAPTER 24
Taking Chances

Kela jolted out of bed and glanced around the bright room in confusion. Her clock read 10:15, much later than she normally got up. Padding across the floor in her bare feet, she peeked out her door. Her father stooped over his toolbox.

"What's going on?" She sat at the kitchen table, rubbing her eyes.

"Sorry. I was trying to let you and Mum sleep in." He continued to rummage. "I needed some nails and knocked over my box."

"Why do you need nails?"

"An animal prowled around the yard last night, but I don't want you to be scared. There are marks on some of the windows, and I want to secure them until I figure out what it was."

Pop grabbed his hammer and walked to the front door.

"Wait!" Kela scrambled for her shoes and followed Pop. A string of blackbirds squawked and chittered from the roof. The ground sloshed and the grass was bent flat from the night's rain. By her parents' window, Kela stiffened. A trail of crushed and matted grass led from the road. Mud streaked portions of the window frame and glass.

"What did that?" Tension twisted in her stomach. Pop pulled out a few nails and began hammering them into the wooden frame.

"I don't know," he said. "Might think it was a crocodile or some other large reptile, but nothing like that is native to St. Rita."

They moved around the side of the house, following the trampled path to Kela's window. Her leaden legs slowed her, and she hung behind Pop. Streaks of mud and grime covered her window too, but there was more damage. The wood had deep gouges, like something sharp had run across the grain. Pop furrowed his brow as he examined it and again hammered nails to secure the window.

"We need to get this one replaced," he grunted as he peered closer at the marks and ran his hand along the wood. "Wish I knew what caused this. I don't like knowing something that can do this kind of damage is loose."

He walked back toward the front of the house, but Kela stayed.

"Come on. I don't want you out here by yourself."

"I'm coming."

Kela moved closer to the window. The streaks did not seem random. She turned her head and thought she could make out the scrawl of letters. *N-O.* She peered closer, and more letters sloped down to the bottom of the pane. *T-I-M-E.*

A rush of wings made Kela look up. A blackbird perched on the edge of the gutter, its yellow eyes fixed on her. Suddenly, its curved beak opened, and it screamed in shrill alarm. The flock rose and fled the roof in a torrent of black wings.

Kela took her hand and wiped her palm across the muddy window, smearing the message.

She ran back into the house as Mum came from her bedroom. Dark circles edged her eyes.

"Mum, are you okay?"

"Bad dream. I didn't sleep well."

"Let me make you some tea."

Mum sank into a chair. Shoulders slumped and her face waxy, the change in Mum over the past two days frightened Kela. She fixed her mother's favorite, ginger tea with honey, and put the cup in front of her.

"Thanks, sweetheart."

"What was the dream about?"

"I—don't know." Mum rubbed her forehead. "There was light. Warm and comfortable, like lying on the sand at Little's Beach. When you close your eyes, you can still see the glow of the sun through your lids. That's how it felt. Peaceful."

"Sounds nice," Kela said. "Why is that a bad dream?"

"I woke up. Although it felt so good there, something pulled on me. I didn't want to leave and fought as hard as I could to stay, but I couldn't. There was nothing to hold on to. I even grabbed at the light, but it was everything and nothing. It got smaller and smaller. When I couldn't see it anymore, I woke up." She stared at her lap. "I've never had a dream that felt so real."

Kela flinched. Her mother's words hit hard and close.

Grief was an ache that wouldn't go away, and Mum's return had filled that void. Her mother being alive again made their family whole, but . . . Kela had never thought about what it would do to Mum.

I did this.

Ophidia had warned her about consequences, but she hadn't cared. Not if she could have Mum back.

What if she couldn't fix whatever was wrong?

Kela wrapped her arms around Mum's shoulders. Warm and alive. She wondered for how much longer.

"Honey," Mum said. "Don't worry. I called in sick to the office and I'm staying home to rest. Run on and do what you were going to do."

"Okay, Mum," she said. "I love you."

"I love you too."

Kela changed her clothes and threw her canvas bag over her shoulder. When she returned to the kitchen, Mum had gone back to her room, and she could hear her talking to Pop. The untouched tea sat cold on the table.

Kela hesitated, then shut the front door behind her.

The heat of the day had already started to set in. Since Pop was staying home with Mum, she worried about her plan. George might be at the dive shop already. She strode toward his house. If luck was on her side, she still might find a clue to where the comb was.

At the center of town, she left the main road and climbed a hill with a cluster of homes at the top. George lived in the house that his parents had built.

Grand in its day, it now sagged on its cinder-block foundation. Chipped paint and a hanging window screen added to its run-down appearance.

Kela crept behind the tree line. George's black SUV was still in the drive.

Hunched, she came even with the house, then dashed across the street to a spot behind the porch. The rattle of the rusty air conditioner blocked any sound from the house. She was taking a chance. It would be almost impossible to hear if someone was coming.

Kela opened a trash can and turned her nose away at the sweltering stench. There had to be clues here. She turned back toward the refuse. She pulled open the plastic trash bag and dumped the trash on the ground. Crumpled coffee cups, guava rinds, sticky flyers from the local resort. When she had finished with the first barrel, she began on the second.

More paper. She unfolded every piece. Mostly receipts from different resorts. And bills. Some were marked with red letters that seemed to be shouting.

As she tried to decipher one paper smeared with a greasy yellow stain, she heard the back door slam loudly.

Kela crouched lower behind the closest trash barrel. George stomped down the stairs carrying a black diving bag, much like her father's, and some gear.

His footsteps came closer and he muttered angrily. "Ah! Them dogs! I'm gonna wring their necks if I catch them." Kela waited in terror for him to come around the side of the can and see her. Instead, he shuffled back to his SUV and threw some equipment into the back. He got in and tossed the dive bag into the passenger's seat.

As George started the engine and backed out of the driveway, Kela held her breath. She couldn't follow without being seen.

George drove away, taking with him any chance Kela had to save her mother.

CHAPTER 25

The Storyteller's Tale

Kela crawled out from behind the trash can. Wiping her hands on her shorts did nothing but add a layer of grit to her palms. She had no leads and no more chances.

Walking to where the car had just pulled away, she noticed a scrap of paper that hadn't come from the pile of odorous trash that perfumed her clothes. She picked it up and smoothed it out. It read "Island Brew. 3."

What did it mean? It felt like too little, too late.

Kela made her way down the familiar sidewalk to Baytown Corner Market. The bell rang and Miss Inniss's voice called out from the back.

"One minute!"

Brushing floured hands on her apron, she came from the kitchen.

"Kela!" she said.

"Can I speak to you and Lissy?"

Miss Inniss's forehead wrinkled with concern. She beckoned Kela to come into the kitchen. Lissy looked up, flour smudging her cheeks.

The room wasn't big but smelled sweet and doughy. Heat wrapped around Kela like a blanket, warm and safe. Miss Inniss opened the oven. She pulled out three pans of sweet bread and turned them out onto a baking rack. She put one loaf on a cutting board and brought it over to the table.

"Talk is best done over a meal," she said. She wrinkled her nose. "Why don't you wash up first, dear." While Kela washed her hands and face in the sink, Miss Inniss cut thick slices of sweet bread and set two on the table for Kela and Lissy. The fragrant odors of coconut and nutmeg filled the room.

Kela realized that she hadn't hurt this Lissy, hadn't pushed her away—because Mum hadn't died in this world. Awkwardness filled her and she felt like she ought to apologize, but it would make no sense. Doing so would confuse Lissy and Miss Inniss more than she already had.

Miss Inniss pulled out a chair and Kela sat down.

"I want to tell you both something and I hope you'll believe me," Kela said.

"What's going on?" Lissy mirrored the worry on her grandmother's face.

"The other day, I asked about seafolk. What if I told you they were real?"

Miss Inniss held her gaze for a long while.

"I believe you," she said. There was no laughter or playfulness in her tone.

"You do?" Kela's eyes widened.

"I've known you all your life. You've never said a word to make me doubt you. If you say that you've seen them, then you have," Miss Inniss said.

Kela closed her eyes and told her story. Some of it they knew, but she filled in the parts they didn't. The words cascaded like a waterfall. She told about Ophidia coming in her dreams, the broken comb, and her wish. So much about the wish.

She wondered how they would take the information about her mother. To everyone else, Mum had not died, but for her, Mum's death was fresh and painful. So was her return. In the end, she explained about the comb being stolen and who she thought had taken it.

When she finished, Miss Inniss wrapped Kela in her arms. Kela looked at Lissy, and her friend reached for her hand and squeezed it tight. Kela still didn't know what to do, but she wasn't alone anymore.

"Love is a powerful thing," Miss Inniss said. "To wish for your dear mother . . ." She drew a deep breath. "You once asked me what I would wish for if I could have anything. I've never met the seafolk, but I do have a story." It was not her usual storyteller's voice and Kela sensed something different in her words.

"My father fished for many years and I missed him sorely when he was away. Many a night, I lay awake wishing he were home.

"Then one day, it happened. My father had an accident on his fishing boat. His leg got caught in a net and he was hurt bad."

Kela and Lissy leaned in as they listened.

"The fishing company sent him home, but paid him enough that we had a little money for the first time in our lives. When he got well, he decided to open a shop instead of going back to fishing. The man that owned this shop was selling and my father bought it."

Miss Inniss had run the market as long as Kela could remember. It was strange to think of it having belonged to someone else.

"My wish came true, but not the way I wanted.

My father made a living running the shop, but he lost something too. He walked with a limp the rest of his life and longed for the sea. He turned to rum to deal with the pain of both."

Sadness entwined her words.

"I loved my father, but you didn't want to be round him when he had been in the drink. I'm not saying he wouldn't have started drinking if he hadn't stopped fishing, but"—she paused—"I wonder even still if I had a part in all that."

Miss Inniss sat back, her hands resting in her lap. "The old women at the church used to say, 'Every rope's got two ends.' It's true, and I've remembered that ever since."

Kela bowed her head with shame. She had heard that saying before. It was an island proverb that meant there was a little good and bad in every choice.

"Do you think I made a mistake?"

"Oh, my dear," Miss Inniss said, "I'm not saying that. You did what felt right to you."

"I would have made the same wish too," Lissy said.

Less than a week ago, Kela had thought magic was the stuff of stories and didn't really exist. Now the world seemed different. Or maybe she was the one who had changed.

"Sometimes, we only see things from our point

of view." Miss Inniss gazed steadily at Kela. "It's in our nature to think of ourselves first. But—and I learned this the hard way—what's best for us isn't always what's best for the people we love."

Sadly, Kela knew this was true. Despair and heartache had been with her since her mother died. She would never have wished that on anyone else, but it was exactly what she had done to her mother when she wished her back.

The pain, fear, and disappointment that Kela had locked inside broke free. They ripped at her mind and heart, tearing down walls. Denial. Stubbornness. Pride. All crumbled until nothing was left but truth.

She understood what the sea woman meant. Magic has consequences. Her shoulders slumped.

"What should I do?"

"Nothing until you get that comb," Miss Inniss said. "Appease the sea woman, then you can deal with this wish."

"How am I going to do that?"

Miss Inniss shook her head. "I've known George Arthur since he was a boy, and he has always been one to take shortcuts. We need to let the police help."

"No!" Kela sat up. "If the police get the comb, I'll never get it back. They'll turn it over to the Ministry."

"You don't know that, dear. In their view, it's still

your father's property."

"How would I get it back from Pop?"

"Talk to him. Tell him the truth."

"I tried that," Kela said, "but he doesn't believe George could have anything to do with this."

"Then you convince him," Miss Inniss said. "If the police learn that George has the comb, your father will listen to you."

Miss Inniss patted Kela with a reassuring hand. "Let me get my purse and I'll drive us to the station house. Lissy, lock the front door and put out the closed sign."

Lissy shot an apologetic glance at Kela, then left the kitchen. Miss Inniss went up the back stairs to her apartment above the shop.

Panic filled Kela. She trusted Miss Inniss, but the police couldn't help and might even make things worse. As she walked to the stairwell, she listened. Miss Inniss was padding around upstairs and would be back any moment.

As quietly as possible, Kela opened the back door and slipped out.

CHAPTER 26

Following the Truth

Dusty tennis shoes pounded the pavement as Kela ran down the alley behind the shops. She paused at the cross street and jumped as Lissy stepped into the open with an exasperated huff.

Before Kela could spit out an excuse, Lissy grabbed her arm.

"Come on!"

She pulled Kela toward the shade of the trees across the street and they scrambled deep under the canopy.

"What are you doing?"

"Gran means well, but you're right. Going to the police isn't the answer."

"You believe me?"

"Of course! I'm in the bushes with you," Lissy

said with a laugh. She squeezed Kela's hand. "I'll help you."

A warmth spread through Kela and she hugged her friend.

"We need a plan," Lissy finally said. "Do you have any ideas?"

"I found this after he drove away, but I don't know what it means."

Lissy unfolded the paper Kela handed her and studied it, chewing her thumbnail like she did when she was thinking. "I'm not sure, but I have a guess. Come with me!"

They crossed the street again and ducked through an alley behind the shops, the shadows cooling the afternoon heat. Boisterous laughter echoed from the local rum shop, where people played a lively game of dominoes. The girls hurried. There was no doubt that Miss Inniss would be looking for them.

At the beach, Lissy walked toward the pier and Kela tugged at her friend's arm.

"Where are we going?"

"There," Lissy said, pointing to the steep wood-planked walkway on the right.

Baytown Harbor Resort crowned the hill, offering its visitors a panoramic view of the harbor, beach, and town. Taxis circled the drive, loading and unloading guests. Lissy ran to the cabstand.

"Hey, Mike!" she said, running up to a parked taxi. "I've got a question."

A dark-skinned young man leaned out the window, turning down the soca music that thumped from his radio.

"What's up?"

"You know this place?" Lissy asked, showing him the note Kela had found.

"Yeah," he said. "That's a coffee shop down in Queensland. Why?"

"We heard it was good," Lissy said with a satisfied smile. "I want to see how their food compares to Gran's."

"Eh, your grannie's got the best sweet bread around. No need to go to Queensland for that."

"Can you tell us where it is?" Kela asked.

"Down on Bailey Street," Mike said. "By the library."

"Thanks!"

Mike nodded and turned up his music again.

The girls ran to the bus stop.

"So three is a time? If it's three p.m., we won't make it," Kela said, still catching her breath.

"Don't say that. We might," Lissy said.

A Queensland bus finally pulled up and they

boarded. Once they were settled in their seats, Lissy continued.

"Gran and I go to the big library now and then, so I know which stop it is. We can ask for directions once we're there."

The bus rumbled up and down winding roads. Kela tapped her feet, willing the bus to move faster. Every time it stopped to pick up or let off passengers, she groaned.

Eventually, they entered Queensland. Lissy rang the bell as they approached the stop for the library.

"Do you know where Island Brew is?" she asked the driver.

"Walk a block to Bailey, then take a right. Can't miss it."

They thanked the driver and got off. After turning onto Bailey Street, they walked only a few meters before Kela spotted a bright orange sign with a coffee bean across the street.

"There it is," she said, ducking behind a nearby tree. A deep brown canopy hung over the entrance. Customers waited in line or ordered at the counter, while others sat at tables.

"Can't see anything from here," Lissy said. "We need to go in, but we have to be careful. If George sees you, he'll know you followed him. I can make some excuse about running errands with Gran if he notices me."

"I should come too."

"You can't," said Lissy firmly. "It's better if you stay here."

"Fine." Kela frowned, but she couldn't argue with Lissy's plan.

Lissy crossed the busy street and entered the coffee shop.

As she waited, Kela imagined George sitting at a table drinking coffee with the jewelry store manager. Were they going to auction off the comb or had the manager found a buyer somewhere? With so many tourists coming and going from the island, if they sold it privately, there would be no way to get it back.

Her feet itched to move, and she scanned up and down the street. Standing around doing nothing was pointless. The line of parked cars along the street sparked an idea. Where had George parked? Maybe he hadn't brought the comb into the coffee shop. Kela bit her lip. She couldn't wait on Lissy's detective work.

Watching for any sign of Lissy or George, Kela trotted down the sidewalk, crouching behind the parked cars. When she reached a side street, she spotted George's black SUV. As soon as she saw it, she sprinted for the driver's side. Most locals didn't lock their cars, and she prayed George would be like Pop and a thousand other St. Ritans. When she pulled the door handle and it wouldn't open, she growled in frustration.

Kela shaded her eyes and leaned in close to the window. Inside the front compartment, she saw empty soft drink cans, old newspapers, and the crumpled wrappers from various snacks. Nothing that proved George guilty of more than having a dirty car.

She moved around the side and peered through the back window. The glass was tinted smoky gray and it was difficult to see inside. Kela squinted hard. There was equipment in the trunk. A computer and printer. Diving gear. Sparks fired in Kela's brain. She was looking at the stolen property from the dive shop.

George would be coming back any moment, and what would Lissy do when she saw that Kela was gone? She had to move.

Running back to the entrance of the alley, she pressed herself against the wall. Kela took a deep breath, then rounded the corner set for a sprint. Instead of sidewalk, she walked into a man's chest. Her breath caught in her throat as she looked up into George's face. And he wasn't alone.

Joyce Callender—her mum's friend—was with him.

CHAPTER 27

Out of Time

"Joyce?" She couldn't understand why Mum's friend would be here—with George. And then her brain clicked. She was the buyer.

"Kela!" Joyce clutched a black bag in one hand, and her eyes darted to the street and back.

George's face twitched and he glanced at his car. Panic flickered in his eyes.

"What are you doing here?" His voice jerked higher than normal.

Kela shifted her feet as she stared. "I'm here with a friend. We're having a day out." Where Lissy was, she didn't know, but Kela hoped she was watching. As she made a move to step past George, he slid over, blocking her path.

"In Queensland?"

"Let's go—" Joyce said in a low voice.

"I can handle it," he said. Joyce glanced at Kela but said no more.

"I—I was in the souvenir shop on the next street," Kela stammered. "The alley is a shortcut, and I'm meeting my friend at the corner."

George laughed nervously. "Is that so? I was afraid you might have followed me."

"Why would I do that?" Kela asked, her words tight and rusty. She inched backward, and her body itched to put space between her and the two adults who blocked her path.

Joyce avoided Kela's eyes.

Kela braced herself to run, but the brash honking of a horn stopped her.

"Look out!" Lissy yelled as she barreled down the sidewalk toward them on a too-big-for-her bicycle. George and Joyce stumbled aside as Lissy skidded into the alley. She yanked the black bag from Joyce's hand and yelled, "Get on!" to her friend.

Kela threw herself over the seat and held on as Lissy pumped her legs faster.

"Hey!" George lunged after them. But they were too fast.

Kela looked over her shoulder. George had broken

into a run and was reaching for his car door. The bike rounded the corner and he was out of view.

A car horn blared and Lissy swerved to avoid it. Kela gripped her friend tighter as they took a sharp turn down a side street and then back onto another main road. Every engine that roared too close she was sure was George's SUV.

They rode for several more minutes, the black bag spinning as it banged against their front wheel. Lissy's deep breathing kept rhythm with the pounding in Kela's chest. She began to relax with each turn of the wheels that put them farther away from the coffee shop.

Eventually, Lissy looked over her shoulder and cranked the brakes. The bike wobbled dangerously.

"Why are you stopping?"

"It's the bus," Lissy said. "We need to get off the streets."

She pulled over sharply and let Kela jump off before letting the bike fall to the ground. Both girls threw their hands up to flag down the Baytown bus that was almost upon them. It screeched to a stop just ahead and the girls ran for the open doors.

"What you playin' at?" the driver said gruffly as they got on board. "The road's not a playground."

"Sorry—thanks for stopping," Kela said as they

quickly paid their fares and found a seat. Other passengers frowned at them with disapproval and annoyance.

They slid into a pair of seats and sank back in exhaustion.

"Do you think someone will steal the bike?" Lissy asked.

"We stole the bike!"

"I know," Lissy said with a frown. "I mean someone else."

Kela understood how Lissy must feel. Sneaking away from home, spying, and now stealing. What else might they do if given a good enough reason?

Lissy pulled out the bag she had taken from Joyce.

"Open it," she said.

Kela took the bag and held it in her lap. Her hands shook as she pulled the zipper.

Relief swept over her. The little wooden box lay on its side. The rusty keyhole stared at her through the late afternoon light. Kela picked it up and opened the lid.

It was empty.

Kela dropped the box back into her lap and leaned her head forward. She couldn't keep the tears from falling. They ran hot down her cheeks and wouldn't stop. Any hope of returning the comb was gone.

Lissy hugged Kela and let her cry. When the tears slowed, a numb emptiness spread through her. Despite everything she had tried, it wasn't enough.

As the bus rocked and bumped along the road back to town, Kela had run out of chances.

CHAPTER 28

Mistakes

When they arrived at their stop, they stepped off the bus and onto the gritty sidewalk. The bustle of midday had been replaced by a sun-painted calm that Kela did not feel. She didn't know what to do.

Lissy tapped her and whispered, "It's Gran."

Kela turned and saw Miss Inniss walking toward them. Her stomach twisted.

"I've been looking everywhere for you." Miss Inniss's voice was tight and her eyes focused like lasers. Kela had never seen her this angry.

Lissy's shoulders sagged, and she and Kela followed Miss Inniss back to her shop. Silence hung in the air like an ax.

Once inside, Lissy started to speak, but Miss Inniss

held up a finger, and her granddaughter instantly fell quiet.

"After you left, I searched in the square and down by the pier. Never had such a worry on my soul!" Miss Inniss shook as she spoke, and Kela's cheeks burned in shame. "Where were you?"

"We went to Queensland to follow George," Kela said quietly. "I'm sorry."

"Sorry is not enough. You were headed for trouble."

"Gran—"

Miss Inniss silenced Lissy again with a single airborne finger and turned back to Kela. "Why would you do that?"

"I—I thought we could find out if George had the comb." Kela bit her lip. Her words sounded naive and ridiculous, even to her own ears. "It was useless."

Miss Inniss sighed and Lissy spoke up.

"In the café, George passed a bag to your mum's friend, then she slid a magazine across the table. There must have been money inside."

"I can't believe Joyce is a part of this," Kela said. "I trusted her."

"She's likely worried too," Miss Inniss said. "If you tell anyone what she did, she will lose her job."

Lissy held up the black bag. "When I grabbed

this, I really thought the comb would be inside."

"I don't understand. George must still have it. He had to have switched the bag somehow. But it doesn't matter. I have to get it back."

"You can't do any more about this on your own," Miss Inniss said firmly. "I'll drive you home, then I'll call the police."

"But they won't help me return the comb to Ophidia."

"No, but you can't return it either right now." Miss Inniss took Kela's hand and squeezed it. "Dear, we all need help."

Kela nodded, but she still didn't agree. The police weren't the help she needed.

She knew she had to tell the truth to the two people she loved most.

When they arrived at Kela's house, an empty drive and dark rooms greeted them. No savory smells came from the kitchen, and the stove sat abandoned against the wall.

"We can stay with you until they come back," Lissy said, but Kela shook her head.

"No, I'll be fine. I need to talk to them on my own."

"Okay, dear," Miss Inniss said. "Remember, though. This is a chance for truth-telling. Not only to your parents, but to yourself."

"To myself?"

"A hard knot of feelings is tangled up inside you. When you look at it close, you'll find a way through." Miss Inniss gave her a tight squeeze. "I'll call later."

Kela sat at the table, staring at her hands and thinking about how everything had gone horribly wrong.

A chance for truth-telling, Miss Inniss had said.

When she made the wish, Kela hadn't seen how it could be wrong. It was natural. But she thought the cost would be hers to pay.

It wasn't. Kela could see the pain in Mum's eyes as she struggled to be the person she once was but couldn't. Pop had also paid a price. He had gone from the terrible strain of one loss to another, unable to pull Mum from her sinking sadness.

The ticking clock on the wall boomed with a hollow echo.

Truth-telling Kela closed her eyes. She remembered the weeks of searching the sand—looking for that missing orange piece for Mum's sea glass collection.

Getting up from the table, she walked into her bedroom and opened a white box that sat on her dresser. Six lovely pieces of sea glass nestled in the bottom—red, yellow, green, blue, indigo, and violet.

Getting back what she had lost had consumed Kela's thoughts. She looked at the rainbow in the box. The truth was that she hadn't been left alone.

Could her mother ever be happy? The answer scared her, as did the possibility that she might lose her again. Ophidia told her magic always came at a price, and Kela was now bankrupt.

If she could still get the comb back from George— she would ask for Ophidia's help, broken comb or not. If she could survive that long. The memory of the gouged windows reminded her that the sea woman might not be in the mood to do her any kindness.

As the sun dropped under the trees, Kela lay on her bed and waited, her mother's rainbow tucked to her chest.

A rattle at the front door finally caused her head to snap up. From the door of her room, she saw her parents come in. Even though Pop's shoulders sagged, he smiled when he saw her.

"Hey, girl. I'm sorry for not leaving a note. I thought your mother might like to take a walk on the beach."

Pop pulled out a chair and Mum sat down.

"How was your day?" Mum asked.

Kela steeled herself, then spoke.

"I need to tell you both something, and I want

you to believe me."

"You know you can tell us anything," Pop said.

"The comb I found"—she hesitated—"it's not some salvage find. It's a sea woman's comb."

"What?" Her father laughed.

Mum didn't say anything, but her brow furrowed as she listened.

"I'm serious. Strange things have happened since I found it, and . . ." She didn't know how to continue. "It's all my fault!"

Her shout stopped her father's laughter, but it couldn't keep the skepticism from his voice.

"What's really going on?"

"I've made a mess of everything!"

"Does this have to do with the robbery? If you know who took the comb, I won't be angry. Just tell me," her father said quietly.

"I found a sea woman's comb in the coral cave!" Kela slapped both hands on the table. "I know it is, because she found me. Her name is Ophidia and she granted me a wish and told me I had to return it to her—or she'd come for me. But when I made my wish, I broke it."

Anger and panic fueled her, and the words she'd been holding back poured out. "But since the comb was stolen, I haven't been able to give it back and she started sending warnings. She's the one who crushed our front yard and tore into our house. I'm afraid something worse is coming."

Her father stared. "I'm not sure what's going on," Pop said, "but if this is from one of those folktales, it's not right—"

"There's more," Kela interrupted. "You should know what I wished for."

The weight of the secret crushed her, so she closed her eyes. The hardest part was coming.

"Mum died three months ago in a car accident, and I wished for her to come back."

The silence in the kitchen was impenetrable. Kela opened her eyes and gazed into her mother's deep brown ones.

"I was—dead?" Mum asked. The words rang hollow in the room.

Pop seemed confused at first, then stood up. "That's an awful thing to say. What's wrong with you?" He pushed his chair away from the table. "We've had a lot of problems, but I never imagined you would say something so absurd. Do you think it's funny to say shocking things like that?"

"No," Kela said, looking down, defeat in her voice. "It's not a joke. Mum was dead and I wished for her to come back."

Pop's face grew tense and he seemed ready to explode when Mum's voice broke in.

"I believe you."

Kela looked at Mum, not daring to accept what she heard.

"Rose!" said Pop. "How can you say that? Don't encourage her!"

Mum sat up and spoke more loudly.

"I believe you. Something has been wrong, and I didn't understand what. I know things and don't remember how. I keep having dreams of someplace else, someplace beautiful. All I can remember is how wonderful it was, and it makes me sad. It's been tearing me apart."

Kela put her hands over her face, covering the joy and pain Mum's words caused her. Then she turned back to her father.

"Pop," she said, her voice filled with urgency, "we didn't go diving this week. Why not?" She pleaded with her father to believe her. "Because Mum wasn't here! You've asked me to go out with you every week for months, but I haven't. Not since she died."

Pop sat still and silent. He had been ready to say something, but his words evaporated.

"You put yourself in danger," Mum said, cupping her hand against Kela's cheek.

"I'm so sorry, Mum," Kela said. "I pulled you back, but something went wrong, and I don't know how to fix it except by returning Ophidia's comb."

Mum took Kela's hands and squeezed them so tightly, and it was like she wanted to take away all of Kela's guilt. Kela squeezed back—and then her father's hands were on top of theirs.

"I don't think I can believe any of this," Pop said with a hoarse voice, "but I'll help."

"We've got to get the comb back."

"If you didn't take it from the shop, who did?" Pop asked.

"George."

"We had this discussion." Pop sighed, and his head slumped back.

"It's him for sure." She spoke quickly to stop Pop from interrupting.

"Lissy and I followed him to Queensland. He met Joyce in a coffee shop, and they made an exchange. Joyce passed him a magazine, and I think money was inside."

"Joyce tried to buy that comb?"

"Yes, but then I made a mistake . . ." Words tangled on her tongue. "Lissy told me to wait for her and I didn't. Instead, I went to check his car. I saw the stolen equipment in his trunk. When I tried to find

Lissy, I ran into George and Joyce. He wouldn't let me leave until Lissy showed up and we got away."

Pop rubbed his forehead.

"The business has struggled lately, but I didn't want to believe anything was wrong." Pop's jaw set in a rigid line and he slammed his fist on the table. "I can't believe he did this!"

"What are we going to do?" Mum asked.

"I don't know. He could be anywhere," said Pop.

"No," Kela said, standing up. "He's going to try to leave the island. We all have to go to the shop—now."

CHAPTER 29
The Storm

The sky turned cloudy and promised another heavy rain. "We've had a streak of bad weather," Pop said.

Kela thought about the recent storms—after she found the box and the night Ophidia gouged her window. What if the one that was coming was like the hurricane of 1667? Her broken promise waved like a tattered flag in the wind.

"It's her," Kela said.

Pop didn't have a response but frowned as he glanced at the sky.

As they drove, she wondered if Miss Inniss had called the police. Would they believe her? Her stomach churned as the truck bounced along the road out of the market square and toward the resort.

The wind picked up and paper and trash whipped along the asphalt as they parked. Pop took Mum's hand and Kela ran ahead down the pier. The weather had wiped out foot traffic on the beach, and only a few stragglers scurried from the shore. An unusual chill cooled the air and an ominous green cast filtered across the sky.

When they reached Blue Water Dive, the *Rose* sat at anchor, its engine idling. No one was aboard.

Pop opened the shop door. The mess from the burglary had been cleaned up, but glassless counters and broken wall displays reflected the damage. Plywood substituted for countertops while the merchandise below lay exposed.

"Why would he do this to his own shop?" Pop asked.

Shuffling sounds came from the back of the store.

"Come on," Kela said.

One of the fluorescent lights in the hallway blinked lazily, ready to burn out. The strobe effect unbalanced her, and she ran her hand along the wall to steady herself. They passed the empty office, then entered the storage room.

George was hurriedly stuffing gear in a large duffel bag.

190

"Hey!" said Pop, eyeing the bag. "We need to talk."

"What are you doing here?" George asked, glancing out the small window overlooking the pier. He gave the contents of his bag a last shove.

"My parents know everything," Kela said.

"Why did you do it?" Pop asked, his fists clenched.

Staring George squarely in the eyes, Kela defied him to deny the truth.

"Hendy, this business has been sinking for years," George said. "Other shops are constantly edging us out. Newer boats, larger staff, shinier equipment. We can't win anymore."

"Why is our bank account practically empty, George?"

"I invested the money in—a business opportunity. I thought it would pay back big, but it was a scam. The people ran off with the money." George looked away. "I couldn't tell you."

Pop bristled. "We're grown men with jobs and families. We can't count on luck to bail us out of our problems!"

"I did it to keep the place afloat. That comb would have fixed everything. Helped me pay back what I lost," George said, rubbing his hand over his head. "I convinced your friend—the museum lady—that we could work out a deal. You hadn't shown the comb to the Ministry yet, and she wanted it, even broken in half, so I told her I could make it happen if she was willing to pay. Keep it in some dusty corner until the robbery had been forgotten. Now she's got cold feet. Said she made a mistake and threatened to turn me in. Said it would be my word against hers." George's voice cracked. "This wasn't supposed to happen."

"There's no way you can sell that comb," Kela said. "Miss Inniss called the police too. They're probably waiting at your house or will be here soon."

"How could you do this, George?" said Pop.

"Do you have to ask, Hendy?" The muscles in his face twitched as he forced out words. "You and your perfect life. My father only left me the business because you agreed to be my partner. How do you think that made me feel? My own father had more faith in a poor kid from across town than his own son."

George's words hit Pop like a blow to the face and he stared at George as if he had never seen him before.

"That is not my fault," Pop said.

George turned his back and zipped his bag closed.

"Please, just give us the comb," Kela said, taking a step forward. "We need it or something bad is going to happen."

George slung his bag over his shoulder and walked toward the door.

Pop looked at his friend with shock and sadness. "Don't go, George. It's not worth it."

Indecision flickered in George's eyes. "I have nothing left. I can start over somewhere else."

George turned and ran out the door. Hope fled with him but Kela couldn't let it slip away.

She darted forward. Ignoring her parents' shouts, she didn't care that she knocked over equipment in her haste.

In the minutes that they had been in the dive shop, the weather had changed drastically. Light had fled the sky and the wind howled. The choppy sea sprayed foam like bitter rain, and she couldn't tell if the salt in her mouth was from the spray or her tears.

George had unmoored the *Rose* but turned in shock when Kela jumped on board.

"Give me the comb!" she shouted over the wind. She lunged for the bag by his feet, but he kicked it away.

"Get off!" he yelled.

"No!" Kela said. "You'll have to take me with you."

The rough waves moved the boat away from the pier, but she wouldn't leave.

The shop door burst open and Pop and Mum ran onto the pier. Pop had a yellow diving tank raised above him as he ran toward the boat.

George whipped around as Pop threw the cylinder through the air. The metal slammed into George's head with a sickening *thud*. He stumbled, crushing Kela with his weight. The wind reverberated with her scream.

Mum jumped onto the drifting boat, stumbled, and grabbed Kela. Pop followed, but the boat lurched on the rough waves. Even before his feet left the pier, it was clear he wouldn't make it. Instead, Pop landed hard in the water, his hands grasping for the railing.

"Pop!" shouted Kela. She and Mum struggled to get past George, but he regained his footing. With one hand grasping his bleeding head, he punched the motor, his eyes wide and hands shaking. Kela and her mother fell back as the boat lurched away from the dock.

Kela knocked her head against the wooden bench next to the control console. She blinked and images swam before her. Mum crouched next to her and called her name.

Pop's shrinking form in the water was the last thing Kela saw.

CHAPTER 30

Monster Unleashed

Crick.

Crack.

This is a story.

Ophidia slipped blessedly back into the cradle of the sea. The grit and decay of the world above the water still contaminated her. She had done what was needed. Yet it was still not enough.

It was too late, and Ophidia's soul was lost. Even now, her body tingled as it began to dissolve. Scale by shining scale, soon she would be no more.

She would not meet death alone.

Greater power awaited her call, and now she

would unleash it. Living on an island, these fragile humans had little to protect themselves from those things that lay buried in the deep. She had gained the key. Now to open the door.

Ophidia swam to the depths of her world. The one whose help she sought had many names, and all were feared. One of the first born of its mother, it had roamed the primordial tides. But its hunger grew without bounds. To protect her other children, the sea had locked it again deep in her womb.

Soon Ophidia would set it free.

As she approached the towering mountain, she searched for the lock. After a moment, she found it. A lightless hole in the craggy face of the stone.

Now the key. Ophidia grasped the jagged tooth in her hand and extended the full length of her right arm into the hole. She pushed the tooth hard into the warm flesh inside.

Excruciating pain shot through her entire body. She screamed, the water silencing her plea, but she did not withdraw. The monster took its payment in blood.

Then the torture ended. Trembling, she pulled her

bleeding arm back from the hole. She closed her eyes to the sight. It would be restored if her comb was returned, though her chances dimmed. For that, the price was a small one to pay.

A rumbling sounded from deep below, and rocks and coral cracked as the mountain moved. Ophidia waited for the door to open.

"Avenge me, sister!"

A creaking roar, like the bending of ancient wood, reverberated. The ocean floor moved as something inside the rock shifted. A monstrosity emerged. Shapeless. Razor teeth without number. It dwarfed the sea woman in its vastness, and Ophidia swam back to give it berth.

Hungry and mouth gaping, it came out of the deep and into the sight of those brave enough to remain. Eyeless though it was, it sensed all. Ascending from the depths, it began its relentless advance toward the islands of men, feeding on anything unfortunate enough to cross its path.

Ophidia bared her teeth through her pain, feeling the tides turn. She clutched her weak and bleeding limb, payment for vengeance. "Nightmare of the deep. Find the betrayer."

The girl hadn't kept her promise, but Ophidia would surely keep hers.

* * *

Crick.

Crack.

The story is put on you.

CHAPTER 31
The Attack

The rolling sway of the cabin and drone of the engine trickled into Kela's consciousness.

"Mum!"

Although her head spun, Kela raised herself from the cot. She was belowdecks on the *Rose*.

"I'm here."

In the weak light, she could see Mum running water in the sink.

The warm closeness of her mother soothed Kela. Mum's hand shook as she laid a cool washcloth on Kela's forehead and stroked her hair.

"How do you feel?"

"Like my head hit a brick wall."

"Close," Mum said. "You did hit your head pretty hard on the bench."

Kela's fingernails pinched the palm of her balled fist, and she forced herself to open it and allow feeling back into her hand.

"Where's Pop?" The memory of Mum's screams still echoed in her pounding head.

"I don't know." Mum spoke softly. "He was in the water—I'm sure he's fine. He's a strong swimmer." She touched Kela's hair again.

Kela struggled to sit up, but Mum gently pushed her back.

"You need to keep still."

"Where are we?"

Mum shook her head. "I didn't see the course George set before he locked us down here, but we're miles from the coast." She leaned in and put her hands on Kela's. "Your father will send help. Every port will be on alert."

"Do you think George will let us go?"

Mum hesitated. "Scared people don't think rationally, but I think we can reason with him."

Outside, wind whistled across the bow, hissing like a cornered viper. Waves slammed against the porthole. Piloting a boat in this weather was foolish, but George was desperate enough to risk their lives along with his own.

The lock on the hatch clicked, but Kela sat up too fast and her head swam.

George sloshed down the steps, breathing heavily, and leaned against the wall. With a trembling hand, he pulled the door shut.

"I'm going to stay down here for a while," George said. He paced in front of the stairs, unable to stand still.

"We have to go back," Kela said. "Pop needs help."

"It's your fault you're here. I just wanted to leave the island."

Kela's gut wrenched as she realized he was right. She was the one who had jumped on the boat, and Mum and Pop had chased her.

"What are you going to do with us?" Mum asked, her steady gaze on George.

"I don't know," he said with a sidelong glance at her.

"Take us back!" Kela begged.

"We're not going back!" A pained expression came over George's face, and his posture deflated. "I might drop you at the next port. That depends on this weather. We'll have to ride it out."

"I've already told you. The weather's not going

to get any better." Kela pointed to the porthole. Outside, a churning gray ocean slammed the hull. The sky swirled in a salty cauldron of mist.

"What are you going on about?" George asked.

"That comb is stolen. It belongs to a sea woman named Ophidia, who told me that if I didn't return it, I would pay a price. And I have," Kela said bitterly. Mum squeezed her hand. "We're all paying the price. This storm isn't an accident, and the only way to get off this boat is for us to throw the comb back into the ocean now."

"You're speaking nonsense," he said. He turned to Kela's mum. "And you're listening to her?"

"I believe her. Have you ever seen weather like this? We hardly ever get heavy rain in St. Rita, but we've had constant storms since Kela found that comb. Other things have happened too . . ."

George raised his shaking hands. "I'm done listening to your made-up fish tales. You'd say anything to get me to turn the boat around. I'm not giving you the comb, throwing it into the sea, or doing anything else but selling it as soon as this storm blows over."

Kela's concentration had been so focused on George that she only now realized that something had changed. The winds stopped. The freakish, unending roar of the storm had hushed, and a sinuous shape slithered across the window, then vanished.

"There's something out there," she said. She narrowed her eyes, and as the lightning flashed, she saw it again. A mottled gray tentacle whipped in the wind, then sank back into the water.

Suddenly, everything in the cabin began to slide. The boat tilted as if it were banking a steep endless curve and they were picking up speed.

"What's going on?" George fell against the stairs. He struggled to his feet and stumbled to the porthole.

"It's a whirlpool—" His voice was drowned out by the wild ocean. "We can't let it pull us in." He ran to the stairs and climbed toward the hatch.

On the other side of the glass, a swirling mass of angry sea churned. Surging waves descended to a convergence of jagged rocks like teeth. As she staggered closer to the window, Kela knew who had sent it.

The rocks at the base of the vortex expanded to expose a bottomless trench into which the water poured. Tentacles, like the one she saw before, lashed in every direction. A creaking roar, like the grinding of a rusty bolt, split the air.

"Don't open the door!" Kela screamed. Her words seemed to stretch as she ran to stop George, grabbing his arm and pulling. "It's not a whirlpool!"

George opened the hatch.

An eternity passed in the fraction of a heartbeat.

The wind tore open the door and George and Kela fell against the deck. As he pulled himself up, a whipping tentacle knocked him flat again.

Kela crawled on her hands and knees and shook her head to clear her senses. She screamed as cold feelers caressed her body. Scrambling on the slippery deck, she had nowhere to hide, and like moths to flame, several more tentacles swayed in her direction. Whatever was in the water had tasted warm, human flesh and hungered for more.

Mottled gray limbs swung across the deck searching for food. Kela scuttled back as far as she could, but there was no escape. A tentacle curled around her ankle and she began sliding across the deck.

"No!" George's shout ripped the air as he grabbed a metal bar and smacked the creature's muscled limb. Flinching in pain, it uncurled and released Kela before drawing back. George reached to help Kela up.

His shout gave the monster another target. Like a volley of arrows, two tentacles shot at him and slammed into his chest; the undeniable *crack* of breaking bones echoed in Kela's ears. They sinuously coiled around George's unmoving body and lifted him up.

Without thinking, she sprang and grabbed his dangling arms. As the creature's limbs carried George higher, Kela held on, muscles quivering. Her body rose above the deck line.

"No!" shouted Mum. She lunged at Kela, grabbing her legs. Kela grunted with her mother's weight, but still they rose. Like a boa constrictor, the creature would never release its prey, and the additional weight of two humans made no difference. In a moment, more tentacles would come to carry them, and the creature would feed.

Despite everything he had done, George had tried to save her. She held on with all her strength, but sweat and sea spray wormed between their fingers.

As the deck drew farther away, his hands slipped from hers.

Kela and Mum tumbled back through the stairwell, landing with a heavy *thud* on the floor of the cabin.

The impact knocked Kela breathless, but she only had moments. She untangled herself and forced her body to take the stairs by twos. With sweaty palms, she yanked the hatch closed and slammed the bolt into place. Kela backed away with wide eyes as heavy tentacles thumped the door. With every *boom*, the door shook. She imagined it flying open and clammy limbs dragging her into the mist.

Despite the force of the blows, the hatch held.

Kela ran to the porthole to see the tentacle holding George sinking back into the open maw of the vortex. The ragged teeth closed, and he disappeared.

"What were you thinking?" Mum cried as she grabbed her tight.

"I tried to save him—"

"Oh, Kela." Mum buried her face in Kela's hair.

Kela let herself sink into the embrace that she had so missed. Despite all the mistakes she had made, this moment also made her remember how she had pushed aside those who loved her. Her father loved her just as much as her mother, and he had been there all along.

A violent *thud* against the hull yanked her attention back outside.

She fought against the force that tried to pin her to the walls and made it to the porthole.

They were not engulfed in the whirlpool yet. The last tentacle still whipped through the air as it retreated into the vortex. The boat spiraled lower toward the rocklike teeth, but the opening contracted. The monster was closing its mouth.

"We're slowing down," Kela realized, and she

clutched at a sudden idea. "Once the tentacles are gone, let's try to start the engines. Maybe we can generate enough force to break free."

Mum frowned, but said, "We can give it a try."

"Once the mouth of that thing closes, let's go," Kela said, her resolve solidifying.

Watching from the porthole, they waited, holding each other close during the dizzying descent. Finally, the last tentacle submerged and the teeth came together like crunching stones.

Kela ran to the stairs, with Mum close behind. As she unbolted the latch, a sound like a demonic trumpet pierced the air, and both covered their ears in pain. The sound ripped and slashed in Kela's mind.

Worse was what followed. An ominous noise rushed and built, like the hurtling roar of a runaway train. She couldn't move or even get out of the way; all she could do was hold on.

Rushing water shot from the vortex and slammed into them, tumbling their boat bow over stern in the relentless rush of the sea.

They screamed, torn away from each other and slammed into walls and floors as the cabin lost all sense of order. Top was bottom, left was right. Kela grabbed a leg of the cot and held tight, anything to stop the spinning world.

That did not keep objects from hitting her. Dishes and utensils from the cabinets, the chair, gear from the cabin. Anything that was not bolted down became a weapon. She lost count of how many times her body turned end over end.

Then, the world shifted.

The boat crashed a last time, upended in the waves.

They were sinking.

CHAPTER 32

Capsized

The *Rose*, her mother's namesake, groaned under the weight of the water that now pressed in from all sides. Parts of the boat creaked and snapped as they gave way to the pressure and absolute silence of the sea.

The water. Insidious in its quiet approach, it would soon drain the heat from their bodies and push the remaining air from the cabin.

"We've got to get out!" Kela shouted. "The water!" The lapping at her feet caressed her skin like icy hands. Trying to sense her position in space, she was disoriented. Instead of standing on the floor, her feet stood on the ceiling. In the bathroom, the toilet and sink hung from above. She was Alice in Wonderland in a world where the rules made no sense.

Mum got on her knees and felt for the opening to the stairs. Now that the boat was upside down, they would need to swim down past the topsy-turvy stairs and then out the hatch to get free.

"The entrance is over here!" Mum shouted over the increasing moans of the boat. Taking a deep breath, she ducked under the water.

"Mum!" Kela got down and groped for the opening through which her mother had disappeared. A splashing gasp and Mum resurfaced.

"It's jammed . . . the door. I couldn't get it open, but it's not sealing either. Water is coming through."

The hatch at the bottom of the stairs was the only way out. If they couldn't get the door open, then they were trapped. The rising water marked time like an hourglass. Their chances for survival shrank as their depth beneath the waves increased. How far had they sunk already?

"Everything that has gone wrong is my fault," Kela said, shivering from the bite of the frigid water. "If I had never touched that comb, we wouldn't be here. You wouldn't be here. Stuck. With me."

Mum sloshed through the icy water and grabbed her tight.

"We're still alive because of you. You didn't know what that comb was when you found it. You certainly didn't cause any of this now. That fault lies with a grown man, one who has paid the price already," Mum said. Kela pictured George's limp form being dragged into oblivion. "We can't give up yet. There must be a way out."

The water in the cabin reached her chest. Kela groped across the room and tried to look out the porthole again. The walls creaked and tiny popping sounds came from the window. She didn't know how long it could resist the crushing pressure building outside. The effects on her own body were real. Her eardrums stretched as the membranes responded to the changing depth outside the boat.

"Mum, do you feel it? I'm not sure we're going to be able to get back to the surface without help. If we had air tanks and could swim out of here right now, we might be all right for a little while, but if we tried to go up too fast, the decompression sickness would be horrible. I don't think we could make it ten feet before our bodies would give out." Her voice wavered as she spoke.

"We'll figure this out," Mum said. "We're strong island ladies and we aren't going down without a fight." She held Kela's chin up and locked eyes with her. "You promise me you won't give up?"

"I won't." Kela wiped the stinging salt water from her face. "We should salvage what we can while we're still able to move and think clearly." The water was coming in fast and was now to her shoulders.

"Let's take turns," Mum said, rubbing warmth into her stiffening fingers. "It's not a good idea for us both to go under."

"I'll go first."

Kela dropped back into the water and kicked to the bottom. She ran her hands over the ceiling, which was now the floor, hoping to feel anything that could be of use. Her hand touched something, and she grabbed it and kicked to the surface.

Bottled water, a lifesaving prize. Kela held it with quivering hands.

She didn't realize how thirsty she was, but the sight of fresh water made her throat clench and her tongue stick to the roof of her mouth. Kela took a small gulp and then Mum took one before screwing the cap back. Pop had told her about the rule of threes for survival. People can survive at least three weeks without food, three days without water, and three minutes without air. As water swashed around her, none of those sounded possible to Kela.

Mum dove and found another treasure: light. The yellow pistol-grip flashlight would make their searching much easier. Orienting it, Kela found the power button. The cabin filled with light so bright, she and Mum closed their eyes briefly. On the side, another switch controlled the intensity, like going from high beams to regular headlights.

"Let's see if it helps us find anything else. Point that at the water while I look," Kela said. Mum held the light on the surface while Kela dove again.

The light made all the difference. It was enough to illuminate most of the submerged space. The water rippled as she passed through, looking beneath overturned furniture and moving objects aside that were broken. She held her breath, listening to the cadence of her heartbeats.

Water soaked into her pores, pruning her hands and irritating the tissues in her mouth. Whether through sapping her body heat or ravaging her skin, the ocean would soon take its due.

Kela was about to resurface when a lump of shadowy black caught her attention. Without the light, she would have missed it.

She swam past the submerged porthole and reached out. With a tug, she pulled the nylon bag free and saw a ghostly gleam through the mesh. Fumbling with the knotted drawstring, she untangled it and looked inside.

It was the comb.

CHAPTER 33
Last Chances

She burst to the surface, gasping and trying to talk.

"Mum, I found it! I found the comb!" She splashed back over to her mother.

"Where?"

Kela showed her the bag with the comb's two pieces nestled inside. The intricate carved zigzags mirrored the waves.

"The bag was jammed in a space by the stairwell. George must have put it there before we got on the boat." The luminous glow of the white surface battled the creeping gloom of the cabin.

Without warning, their world rocked again. Broken and battered, the vessel lolled to the side, and more water came rushing in. The icy water did little to buffer the crunching jolt. Kela spluttered and tried to keep her head above water. The air bubble, though smaller, remained above their heads.

She still clutched the bag with the comb, but she struggled to hold it and tread water. Mum went under and Kela screamed for her. After seconds that seemed like eons, her mother broke the surface and gasped, dragging air into her frayed lungs.

"What happened?" Kela said. She swam toward Mum, afraid of losing her.

"I think we hit bottom," said her mother. "We're not moving anymore."

Their downward descent had stopped. Only the moaning groans of a dying boat echoed. The *Rose* had been claimed by the sea and now lay in its final resting place.

Ophidia had done what she had vowed. She had dragged Kela to the bottom of the waves.

Mum untwisted the flashlight strapped to her wrist. As she flipped it on, the glow illuminated the landscape below their kicking feet. The cabin was almost filled with water and would soon become a steel tomb.

Kela wondered how long she could tread the freezing water. Mum dove, and she watched the light move toward the stairway. After several bangs below her, the light got brighter as Mum returned.

"The door's still jammed." Water sputtered from Mum's lips as she spoke. "If we could get it open, we'd probably have to move sand to squeeze out."

Trembling, either from the cold or from the deepening knowledge that she was going to die here, Kela listened. Her arms ached and fatigue settled in her bones.

"Come on," Mum ordered. "I have an idea."

She lifted the flashlight and shone it above the water. Across the cabin was the narrow opening to the restroom.

"Go in there and grab on," her mother said when they reached it. Kela moved forward, the bag with the comb still tight in her grasp. The toilet hung highest on the ceiling, and its round bowl gave her something to wrap her arms around.

"This is kind of gross," Kela said with a grimace, "but at least it's something to hang on to." Her leg muscles relaxed, and she allowed her arms to do the work of keeping her head above water. "What about you, Mum?"

"I'm fine," she said. "If I get tired, I can hang on to the door." She moved to the side and grabbed on. It wasn't as good as the support Kela had from the toilet. The sliding door panel was slick, and there was no knob to leverage a foot on. Kela pretended that she didn't notice so Mum would be satisfied.

"We have the comb," Kela said through quivering lips. "Ophidia said all I had to do was throw it back into the sea."

"It's broken. Do you think it will still work?"

"It's the only chance we have."

Mum eyes flitted around the dusky waters of the cabin. Her voice shook.

"It's trapped in here with us. Your sea woman doesn't have it yet."

"Maybe she'll help us," Kela said. "I mean, if she frees the comb, she'll also free us."

Mum nodded, but Kela knew she didn't share her optimism.

Kela closed her eyes. The sloshing water in the cabin and the sighs of the boat grated in her ears as she rested her face against the stainless steel of the toilet bowl.

They waited. There was no way to tell time, but it seemed endless. Limiting talking conserved strength and oxygen. Mum alternated between treading water and using the doorframe to keep herself afloat. When she bobbed lower in the water, she kicked up, but tired muscles were taking their toll.

After what could have been hours, new sounds

echoed through the water. Squeals, pipes, thuds. Kela's eyes widened. The noises set her teeth on edge. Not the moans of the boat—these were coming from outside.

They were not alone.

"We're in here!" Kela began shouting. She banged her fist against the bathroom wall, hoping someone would hear.

"Wait," her mother whispered. "I don't think those are people."

Kela began to imagine what might be circling the boat. Creatures that never surfaced and lived off the dead or dying.

She thought she knew the ocean, but she was in another world. A world with seafolk and monsters. A world she might not survive.

Mum rested her head against the door, her eyes closed. Her body trembled from fatigue and her grip kept sliding.

A shrill scraping along the hull startled them, and there was only one possible cause: sharp claws and pent-up hate.

"She's here!" Kela reached toward Mum. "Quick! I need the flashlight."

Once she had it, Kela took a breath and dove below the surface. Fear tangled with nervousness as she swam toward the porthole.

On the other side of the murky glass, midnight loomed. For a moment, a flash of scales streaked by and then nothing. Kela pressed her face against the window, struggling to see more.

A face sprang from the darkness. Ophidia slammed against the window and hissed with venom.

Kela gasped and water choked her. Struggling, she kicked up and sputtered in the stale air.

"Kela!" Mum screamed.

"I'm okay." She dragged in air in broken breaths. She took another deep breath and went under again.

At the window, Ophidia's hair trailed around her snake eyes, but Kela shrank back at what else she saw. Gray film clung to her mottled skin, and yellow patches crusted her gills and scales. Ragged tatters of her tail fin drifted in the current.

Kela held up the diving bag and pulled out the pieces of the comb. Ophidia hissed again, then vanished into the place between light and shadows.

Kela kicked up to the surface and gasped as air rushed into her lungs. The lack of oxygen made her chest tight as she splashed over to Mum.

"What is she doing?"

Kela's voice shook. "I don't know."

They waited for any sign that Ophidia understood.

A sign that help was coming.

A *boom* shook them both and the boat rocked. Pointing the flashlight toward ripples by the staircase, Kela waited. A heavy force slammed against the boat again, and the hatch that had been jammed exploded out of the water and into the cabin. A surge of water rushed in, and Kela and Mum worked to keep their heads above it.

The door was open.

CHAPTER 34

Past, Present, Future

A shadow passed through the stairwell and moved sinuously through the water. Glints of green and gold broke in sprays.

The sea woman hissed, defiant in her wretched state. Breath rattled in her throat, and foam drifted from her dissolving body.

Kela faltered in the grip of Ophidia's pitiless gold eyes.

"It's here. I tried to return it—"

"Liar!" Ophidia said. "You broke my comb!"

"Not on purpose. Please believe me!" Kela begged, but she stopped. Nothing she could say would matter. "I'm sorry. I wish I could fix it." She held out the comb to the sea woman.

"Human, you will rot at the bottom of the sea. When I am nothing but foam, your bones will still lie, bleached by the salt of my mother's tides."

Ophidia reached for the pieces of the comb in Kela's hand. As her webbed fingers closed around them, the fragments throbbed with a blue light. Kela tried to pull away, but she couldn't. Ophidia stared, as if she too didn't know what was happening. The glow engulfed their hands. Then it vanished.

The comb was whole.

Before Kela could say a word, the water around Ophidia shimmered. Gray film and crusty patches of skin sloughed away. Limp, drowned hair sprang into inky locs, and her radiant brown skin and scales shone again with a terrible beauty.

Kela broke free at last and splashed toward Mum. Her mother clutched her tight.

Ophidia stared at her comb as if she were seeing it for the first time.

"How did you do this?" she asked. The anger that had radiated from her had been replaced with confusion.

"I—I didn't do anything," Kela said. "I swear. But you have magic. Right?"

"Not this kind," Ophidia said slowly. She turned

the comb in her hand. "This comb once belonged to another. As long as I keep it, I may live. Once it is broken, though, its magic fades. I cannot repair it."

"I don't understand," Kela said.

Ophidia studied her. "Seafolk are not born with souls. We must take a human soul or die when our days are done. I claimed a soul and put it in this comb."

"But whose soul is it?"

Ophidia tossed her head, and the black slits of her eyes narrowed. "A girl I thought a friend. She betrayed me, just like you."

A strange feeling welled in Kela. Bits and pieces clicked together. The family story and the orange-clothed girl from her vision.

"Meera," Kela whispered.

Ophidia's head jerked up. "How do you know that name?"

"My great-grandmother told me about her. A distant aunt who was lost at sea," Mum said. "The story has been passed down for generations in our family. Her name was Meera."

Ophidia's eyes widened. "Then that is how the comb was restored. The bond of blood holds powerful magic."

"You mean I have magic?" Kela breathed.

"Of a sort," Ophidia replied. "The comb needed us both."

"Wait—you need to know the truth," Kela said to the sea woman. "I didn't betray you. And neither did Meera. Her mum was being auctioned away from the island and her papa wanted to buy her freedom. Meera didn't know her papa's plan."

Kela glanced down at the ghostly comb Ophidia clutched in her long fingers. "That belonged to her?"

The sea woman nodded.

Ophidia's voice was low and barely audible over the dying groans of the boat.

"I kept it and bound her spark of soul to it." Ophidia held the comb to her chest, water dripping like tears. "I thought her a traitor."

"She wasn't. She tried to save you."

Creaking silence swallowed them again. For seconds, the only sounds were the groans of the hull and the slaps of water against the cabin walls.

"Meera was my only friend," Ophidia said, looking at Kela and Mum. "Losing her—changed me."

"But she's still with you." Kela gestured toward the comb. "She's been with you from the beginning."

She studied Ophidia and thought she could see a glimpse of who Meera had befriended.

"You want something," Ophidia said. Her face

so close, Kela could feel the cold current of the sea woman's breath on her cheek.

"Not for me—" Kela said.

Ophidia's eyes swallowed Kela in their bottomless black. Kela's heart hammered as she tried to find the words.

"Mum's not the same—" Kela searched for an explanation. "She's lost . . . on the inside."

Ophidia's expression hadn't changed, but gold flickered in her eyes.

"Magic always has consequences." Ophidia glanced at Mum. "The connection between life and death is deep, and sometimes magic cannot altogether overcome it."

Kela tried to make sense of Ophidia's words, but they were a jumble.

"She is trapped between worlds. Between this and that which lies beyond. Her body returned but her soul could not."

Kela thought about her mother's dream of being pulled away from the light. Was that what it felt like to be ripped away from your soul?

Ophidia turned to Mum. "You know that I speak the truth."

"Yes," Mum said. "I don't know how . . . but I do."

"I wished for Mum to come back." Kela shivered

in the frigid waters. "I did this." Ophidia's face was still impenetrable.

"One is not whole when a piece is missing." The jagged white tines of the comb grinned from her hand.

Ophidia's storms, nighttime summons, dangerous wishes, and exacting vengeance began to make sense and swam in Kela's thoughts. The rippling weight of her decisions pressed down.

"I'm sorry for what I've done," Kela said.

Ophidia studied the girl. "You are the first to ever say those words to me."

"Then I'm even more sorry."

"You still have not said what you want."

"Please. It's all my fault. Mum doesn't deserve to suffer for my mistakes."

"What does any of us deserve?" Ophidia arched her head and her snake eyes glimmered.

Kela hung her head.

"You told me the truth about Meera," Ophidia said slowly. "For her, I ask this. What would bring you happiness?"

Kela froze. It was not a question she had expected, but she recalled being asked it before. It seemed so long ago.

Every moment of the past few days had changed her. Until she had found the comb, all she could think about was Mum and wanting her back. She made that wish come true, but at a deep and painful cost.

An answer rose to her lips.

"I only want Mum to be happy again. That will bring me happiness."

With a powerful flick of her tail, Ophidia dove below them.

Kela pointed the flashlight and tracked the sea woman's lithe form. Ophidia touched the small mirror in the bathroom, and it shifted to a wavering pane of light. She traced its edges and it expanded.

Cold spray splashed their faces on Ophidia's return. "You have only to touch the surface," she said.

"Thank you!" Kela's heart swelled as she realized the happiness their escape would bring Mum. She pulled on her mother's arm. "Let's go."

Mum did not move toward the portal. Her brow was furrowed in thought.

"You said, 'One is not whole when a piece is missing.'"

Ophidia's unblinking eyes gazed at Mum as she spoke.

"I am not whole."

Kela didn't understand why Mum was asking this now. They had a way to get home.

"What will happen to me when I go through

that?" Mum asked.

"Humans cannot live in this world without a soul."

"What's been happening to me will get worse."

"Eventually, you will cease to hope and fade to nothing," Ophidia replied.

Kela's mouth parted as understanding cut through her. Ophidia had said her mum's body had returned but her soul hadn't. This was the result. How much time would they have when they got back to the other side?

"I want you to stay with me," Kela sobbed.

Mum smiled sadly.

"I want to . . . but I can't." She caressed Kela's face.

"Mum—"

Her mother shook her head. "I love you and am so proud of you."

"But what about Pop?"

"He'll be all right. You both will. You'll be together."

The shimmer from below cast eerie shadows up through the water. Kela hugged Mum. The sweetness of escape was gone, leaving only the inescapable truth of what going back meant. Losing Mum again would be more painful than anything she could imagine.

Ophidia had not spoken, but Kela glanced toward her and noticed she had turned away. Her comb close to her face, she seemed to be speaking to it.

"For centuries I have dealt with humans," Ophidia said at last. "I have seen selfishness and greed time and again. There was no more for me to know." She turned to face them again and her snake eyes were bright. "Or so I thought."

Kela quieted her breathing so she could take in the words.

"You cannot resume your former life, Rose Boxhill. Without a soul, you will grow more listless and fade to nothing. I offer you another choice."

"What choice?" Kela asked.

"A grace. A gift my kind may bestow only once. There was only one other I would have considered worthy. It is fitting that you carry her blood. If you accept, you can have a life in the sea with a new soul. Sharing mine." She held out Meera's comb.

Mum's mouth parted in surprise.

"As one of the seafolk?"

"Yes," replied Ophidia.

A slow smile spread across Mum's face. "I accept."

Then Ophidia smiled, not the dangerous kind, but one of friendship and trust.

Joy leapt in Kela. "Mum, we can still be together! I could meet you by the sea or talk to you through a mirror."

Ophidia watched, but she gave a barely percep-
tible shake of her head. Mum closed her eyes for a
long moment. "I've read enough stories to know,
Kela. Landfolk and seafolk aren't supposed to be
together."

"But it could be a secret. No one would have to
know . . ." Kela trailed off as she noticed Ophidia's
face. Tears stung her eyes again, but she understood.

"Remember," Mum said. "Even if you can't see
me . . ."

"You're there," Kela said. Her voice hitched. "You
won't forget me?"

Ophidia answered. "No, Kela. The sea does not
forget. Your mother will remember you as long as
the tides rise and fall. And so will I."

Kela stared into Ophidia's golden eyes and wres-
tled with what to say. Then she looked at Mum, her
brown eyes tender and loving.

"Mum—"

"I love you."

Ophidia spoke again and her gills fluttered softly
like wings. "Kela, your way is through the portal.
Do not delay."

"Where will it take her?" Mum asked.

"To safety. She will find what she needs on the

other side." Ophidia held out her hand to Mum. "Take my hand, Rose. We must go as well."

Ophidia's gold eyes were no longer cold, but warm like the most brilliant amber sand.

Mum hesitated, then took Ophidia's hand, and the sea woman gripped it tight. Then Ophidia began to sing. Not a mournful song—the sea woman's voice soothed and filled Kela with peace, even as pain pierced her heart.

The spark of soul in the comb glowed again and encircled Mum in its luminous light. She was more beautiful than Kela had ever seen.

With a tremendous splash, Ophidia and Mum dove. They swam below the surface, tail and legs kicking straight down.

Through the stairwell and out the open hatch, they swam. Kela dove then watched from the porthole as the silhouettes, two forms—hands clasped—drifted away from the boat. The brightness around them pulsed and Kela covered her eyes.

When she looked again, there were not two, but three shapes. Kela pressed her face against the glass. The third clasped hands with the others, her tail a flash of orange amid their green and gold.

Ocean silt spun like clouds from the forceful

motion of their tails.

They were gone.

Kela turned toward the mirror. The portal shimmered, guiding her way forward. She reached out to touch it, the surface warm and inviting to her fingers. Gripping the edges of the frame, she pulled herself through.

CHAPTER 35

The Gift of Grace

Kela squinted, her senses grasping for any familiar shape or sound. Her feet stood solidly on a dry floor and she reached out to feel anything that might be real. Objects and noises sharpened into focus. The hard angles of a dresser. The matchbox outline of a bed. The comforting smell of coconut oil.

She was home.

Magic had brought her to the place she most needed to be. No decompression sickness, no peeling skin from hours in the sea. Her mother's wish had come true.

Kela felt something at her throat and reached up to feel the orange sea glass necklace Ophidia had worn. A mermaid's tear. She understood it now.

She found the cool smoothness of her bedroom door and turned the knob.

Like magnets, her feet drew her toward the living room and to the tall bookcase. Kela took the worn book of folktales from the shelf and sank into the creaking softness of the couch. Waves of sadness rose inside her. Tears stung and she hugged its blue cover like a long-lost friend.

So much had happened and she felt so very tired. Kela wanted to sink into a dreamless sleep. And yet . . .

This moment felt oddly familiar. Like she had been here, done this before. But she hadn't. Had she?

Clutching the book, she got up and entered the kitchen, trying to find words for her strange feeling. She looked around the room. Faint light trickled through the window curtains. A coffee-stained mug and a plate rested in the sink. But on the table she saw it.

The pale wrinkled sheet of paper.

She picked it up, and in her father's blocky print she read:

Let's take a dive today.
Love, Pop

It was the note that Pop left the morning she had found the comb.

Kela's mind spun. She glanced at the book clutched in her hands. This was her second chance. Not only Ophidia's grace, but Meera's.

She didn't know how it was possible, but she didn't care. She'd soon go to the dive shop and give Pop the biggest hug she could.

With a start, she realized something else. George was alive. Several voices chattered in her head—but she could hear Mum's voice the clearest. In the end, he had saved her life.

She needed to talk to her father, to make it all right, but there was something she wanted to do first.

The sun bathed the island in a warm embrace, and the sky mirrored the playfulness of the sea with clouds like flossy whitecaps. In town, tourists crowded the streets. The air was thick with rich smells and music that lifted the feet and the soul. St. Rita was alive.

She walked, her satchel bouncing at her side. What she had to do next was hard, but after everything that had happened, she could do it.

As she approached Miss Inniss's shop, Kela spotted Lissy sweeping the sidewalk. She had so much to tell her.

"Lissy!"

Lissy looked up in surprise.

"I'm sorry I've pushed you away," Kela started quickly. She was afraid that if she stopped, she might not be able to say what she needed to. "It's been hard with Mum being gone, and—" Kela's voice hitched.

Lissy dropped the broom and wrapped her arms around her friend. Kela sank into a deep, overwhelming sense of relief and returned her friend's embrace.

"I know."

"You know?" Kela pulled back in bewilderment. "Know what?"

"Everything. It's strange. I woke up this morning and it was like I could remember different versions of the past few days. I remember what we did—and about your mum."

Kela's eyes widened in shock. This was another gift.

"I promise I won't abandon our friendship again."

"Good, because I won't let you either." Lissy pushed Kela playfully.

"I need to tell you something important." Kela took off the orange sea glass necklace and pressed it into Lissy's hand.

Lissy's eyes widened. "But how?" she breathed.

"I'll tell you, but it'll take some time. You'll need these." She pulled out her mother's notebook and recorder and handed them to Lissy.

Kela pulled up one of the chairs in front of the shop and took out her well-worn book of folktales. Lissy looked puzzled but sat next to her.

"Do you remember the vision I saw when I touched the comb, the girl in the orange skirt?"

"Yeah, sure."

"Well, I have more to tell you. Who she is. Why the comb called to me back in the cave." She gestured for Lissy to turn on the recorder. "And it starts with that," she said, pointing at the sea glass in her friend's hand. The fragment of glass glowed brightly.

After a pause, Lissy's mouth formed its familiar smile. She hesitantly opened the notebook and took up the pen tucked inside. She clicked the red button on Mum's recorder. Miss Inniss walked to the door, wiping her hands on her apron, and leaned against the frame to listen.

Kela took a deep breath.

"This is a story."

CHAPTER 36

Return to the Sea

Kela's scuba mask pressed soft and warm against her face, and the warm Caribbean sun bounced off the surface of the sea.

The imaginary tightrope she had been walking on for months had burned away. There was no need for balancing acts and routines anymore. If she fell, she knew the people who loved her would catch her.

"Are you ready?" Pop rechecked the straps on her equipment, his ebony hands rough and strong.

"I think so."

"I'm not," said Lissy. Her friend bit her lip and looked sideways at Kela. "You promise not to leave me on my own down there?"

"Only because you promised to come with me to the Creative Arts Program," Kela said. Storytelling was part of the narrative arts, and it hadn't surprised Kela when Lissy won a scholarship.

Lissy's eyes brightened. "Pinkie promise," she said, hooking Kela's finger with hers and squeezing tight.

"You girls were born ready," Miss Inniss said, coming up behind them. She squeezed her granddaughter reassuringly on the shoulder.

Pop tightened Lissy's straps. "All set." Kela smiled at him from over her shoulder.

Now Kela rested on the gunwale of the boat. She released her grip and flexed her stiff fingers.

"Take your time. Lean into the rhythm of the water," Pop said softly.

Kela leaned forward, teetering against the heavy tug of the bright yellow scuba tank.

Tucking her chin and holding on to her mask and regulator, she let the weight of the tank flip her backward into the warm Caribbean.

Panic grabbed her as she hit the water. The dizzying somersault lasted only a moment, but not the feeling of being dragged down. Years of practice couldn't stop her arms and legs from flying out, refusing to be swallowed. She made herself stay calm, not fight, and relaxed into the sea's embrace.

Exhaling long and slow, Kela emptied her lungs and her body dropped. She touched her side to make sure her dive bag was still there. And, more importantly, what was inside.

Meter by meter, she adjusted the speed of her descent. Lissy had entered the water just after her and floated above. Kela repeated the breathing process until the dive computer on her wrist displayed their chosen depth.

Fish darted like silver bullets beneath the surface. Fifteen meters above her, the ceiling shimmered of glass and light, and she delighted in the absence of sound. No splashing or shrill bird cries pierced this side of the water. Nothing except what she had brought with her: the movement of her body through the water, the rhythmic intake of her breathing, and the percussion of her heart.

When she was little, Kela had learned to snorkel with Mum and Pop along shallow reefs off St. Rita's coast. When Mum died, she couldn't bring herself to come back. Now Kela felt her in the warm currents and in every ray of light.

Lissy matched her depth and Kela swam to her. The underwater forest pulsed in a kaleidoscope of color and texture.

They watched a scavenging spotted cleaner shrimp, flying gurnards with their winglike fins, sandpapery filefish with their neon scrawls, and sharp-angled jackfish. Lissy peered into a crevice, and unblinking eyes stared back. A green moray eel, razor teeth gaping, swayed its head. Lurching back, Lissy and Kela kicked away. The eel snaked forward, muscles rippling over the rough coral.

The reef was its home, and they were the strangers. Keeping their eyes on the moray, they changed direction.

Kela eventually signaled to Lissy and turned toward open waters. Kela swam above the rocky landscape, working to keep her body horizontal.

Treasures carpeted the ocean floor, but they weren't here to take. They had come to return.

With Lissy by her side, Kela reached into her dive bag. Inside was the gift magic had let her keep.

She pulled out the delicate orange sea glass necklace. A mermaid's tear. Not of sadness, but of joy. This time it dangled from a vibrant blue crocheted chain that she had made. Pretty enough for a mermaid to wear.

She removed two more necklaces from her bag; translucent companions in green and amber with chains of gold metallic thread. Never had Kela worked so carefully. Never had it meant so much.

Where was Mum now? Kela's heart ached for her mother, but it also brimmed with fullness and peace.

I know you wanted me to be safe and I am, she thought. Pop's all right too. She paused as she gathered her words.

Mum—I hope you don't mind if our rainbow stays the way we left it. I want you to have this.

Kela clutched Mum's necklace in her hands and poured all her love into it. She laid it gently on the sand in the shelter of the reef. She then placed the other necklaces beside the first, a trio of diffused light in the shadows.

Somehow it would find Mum. She knew this in her heart.

Kela. Mum. Ophidia. Meera.

The sea had brought them together—connected them—and it always would.

She signaled a thumbs-up to Lissy to indicate that she was ready to go.

In matched strokes, they kicked skyward toward the bright ball of light above. Kela knew she had made the right choice this time.

Crick.
Crack.
The story is put on you.

A Note from the Author

I say Crick, you say Crack.

Crick.

Crack.

This is a story.

A Comb of Wishes is about the power of stories. Woven within its pages is a history: of a girl, her family, and her culture. That girl is both Kela and me.

The truth of storytellers, and who can tell a story, ripples through this book. I wrote the beginnings of *A Comb of Wishes* in November 2013, during my second attempt at NaNoWriMo. I had just completed my master of arts in education degree at Michigan State University, having returned to school after fifteen years in the classroom. At the encouragement of a friend, I had resumed my interest in writing and began to study the craft.

One of my takeaways from my study of children's literature in graduate school was knowledge of the dearth of published books by BIPOC creators. Recent statistics reflect that just 5 percent of children's books published are by Black creators. Even when those books are published, often they are not given the visibility and support needed to make sure they find their way to readers. Even in my own classroom, a curriculum audit revealed my lack of inclusion of voices of color. I am embarrassed and ashamed of my past oversight and have committed to do better, which I have. But I also wanted publishing to do better. As Dr. Rudine Sims Bishop notes, "When children cannot find themselves reflected in the books they read, or when the images they see are distorted, negative, or laughable, they learn a powerful lesson about how they are devalued in the society of which they are a part."*

---

*Bishop, Rudine Sims. "Mirrors, Windows, and Sliding Glass Doors." *Perspectives: Choosing and Using Books for the Classroom* 6, no. 3 (1990), scenicregional.org/wp-content/uploads/2017/08/Mirrors-Windows-and-Sliding-Glass-Doors.pdf.

In writing *A Comb of Wishes*, I hoped to create a book that a twelve-year-old me would have wanted to read. A voracious reader growing up, I loved fantasy and read books like the Chronicles of Narnia and *A Wrinkle in Time*, yet I never saw myself in the pages of those stories of the fantastic. I wanted to write a character who kids would find relatable and real. Smart, but flawed. Brave, but scared. Willing to do the right thing when it counts. Someone that all kids can root for, but with whom Black kids especially could identify. In crafting Kela, this book also became a story about my family and my Caribbean heritage.

My father emigrated from Barbados to the United States in 1967 and raised me in a vibrant West Indian immigrant culture in Boston, Massachusetts. Calypso and soca played at family events, and peas and rice, plantains, saltfish cakes, and oxtail graced our table. Much of my own father can be seen in Kela's pop. He was a man who loved the sea, diving, and spearfishing, but who also loved his family deeply. Even though he passed away shortly before this book was acquired for publication, he knew about the story, and I am certain he would be proud of what it has become.

Much of my paternal grandmother is also woven throughout the story—including her name, Rose. Both Kela's mum and Miss Inniss reflect the best parts of her, most notably her cooking, her love of conversing, and her generosity of spirit.

Finally, *A Comb of Wishes* is a story about loss and the love that remains. The COVID-19 pandemic has brought grief and sadness to many families. Many of us have been separated from loved ones in order to keep one another safe, and others of us have said goodbye to those we love due to the virus. I hope Kela's story brings comfort to those who have experienced such losses. Her story is one that acknowledges that pain while recognizing the precious gifts left behind by those we love. In an early draft of the novel, Kela collects and makes jewelry from seashells. After feedback about the environmental harm caused by recreational shell collecting, I changed Kela's hobby to collecting sea glass. It was only later that I learned the folklore behind these beautiful gems. Mermaids' tears—sadness turned to beauty—seem an appropriate metaphor for this moment.

I hope this story finds its way to its readers and fills a much-needed place on the bookshelf where Black and brown children can see themselves swimming with mermaids and making their wishes come true.

Crick.
Crack.
The story is put on you.

Sincerely,
Lisa Stringfellow

Acknowledgments

The heart of this story is based on the influence of my family, some of whom have left us. I miss them all dearly. To Dad, Nanny, Pappy, and Uncle Roger, pieces of you are in this book.

Mom, thank you for being a well of support throughout my life. Dudley, thank you for being the most talented person I know and a kind and generous human being.

To my children, Michaela, Benjamin, and Althea, thanks for being yourselves. I love you!

To the Bryans and Simmonses, my large and loving Bajan and Southern extended families: Your support and encouragement mean everything.

To my agent, Lindsay Auld: Thank you for your support and encouragement, keen editing eye, and faith in this story.

Thank you to the hardworking team at Writers House, who supported my book from the beginning: Steven Malk, Cecilia de la Campa, and Aless Birch.

To Rosemary Brosnan, I feel blessed to have you as an editor. Your guidance helped this story become its best self. I appreciate your endless support.

Thank you also to the wonderful and passionate team at HarperCollins and Quill Tree Books: Suzanne Murphy, Courtney Stevenson, Lindsay Wagner, Ivy McFadden, Andrea Pappenheimer and the HarperCollins sales team, Vaishali Nayak, Delaney Heisterkamp, Patty Rosati, Mimi Rankin, Katie Dutton, David Curtis, Erin Fitzsimmons, Vanessa Nuttry, Sean Cavanagh, and Jacquelynn Burke.

Michael Machira Mwangi: I am beyond words. Thank you for lending your amazing talent to the cover.

This book would not be what it is without the guidance of my mentors, Robin Yardi and Sarah Ahiers. Thank you, Robin, for helping me find my middle grade voice. Thank you, Sarah, for pushing me to develop Ophidia's character and complexity.

Thank you to Justina Ireland for accepting me

in Writing in the Margins and for connecting me with Robin. Thanks also to Alexa Donne of Author Mentor Match for connecting me with Sarah and for encouraging me to accept both mentorships that I was offered.

Kelly Barnhill: Thank you for *so* much. For connecting me with Lindsay, for reading my manuscript, and for writing the most amazing words about it. You gave me the courage to write an unconventional middle grade novel with a three-hundred-year-old mermaid as a POV. It was the way the story needed to be told. Before reading *The Girl Who Drank the Moon*, many told me "that's not the way it is done." Thank you for showing me that it could be.

To Laura Pegram and Kweli: You are a light. The Kweli Color of Children's Literature Conference was the first affinity space for BIPOC kidlit creators that I found. My humble appreciation for honoring me with the inaugural Kweli Color of Children's Literature Manuscript Award in 2019. Thank you also to Leah Henderson for your support and personal encouragement. I am grateful to the many authors and creators I learned from during Kweli master classes, including Rita Williams-Garcia and Renée Watson.

Thank you to the SCBWI Midsouth and New England regions for welcoming me and helping me grow as a writer.

Writing is often stereotyped as a solitary activity, but that is not the truth. Writers need a community to sustain them. Thank you to my critique group, the Wordsmiths: Ashley Storm, Allison Russell, April Roberson, and Sherry Howard. Your kind guidance and unending encouragement have meant the world to me. Thank you to Erica Rodgers, who suggested the idea of a "mermaid's grace." Thanks to Kristine Asselin, my query godmother. Thank you to my fellow authors of the #22Debuts, KidLit in Color, the Brown Bookshelf's Amplify Black Stories Cohort, and Black Creators in KidLit for your nurturing support.

Inked Voices: Thanks to Risa Nyman, Ann Matzke, and Tamra Tuller. You were the first to read the entire manuscript. Thank you to Word by Word, who kept me accountable and grounded as a reader and writer: Brooke McIntyre, Heather Pagano, Pauline Mountain, Meagan Fong, Gail Schwartz, Mistina Bates, Julie Fas, and Andrea Appleton. Thanks to Christine Carron for our lunches and book talks.

Savvy Authors: In 2013, I signed up for the NaNoWriMo Boot Camp. I'm eternally grateful to Lyndsey Davis, my team captain and cheerleader. I'm also grateful to Rhay Christou, who encouraged me to keep writing after the wind was knocked from my sails.

To my "book bubbe," Sarah Aronson: Your generosity and support are a gift. Thanks to the writers in your classes who shared such helpful feedback, including Thornton Blease, who kindly pointed out the negative environmental impact of shell collecting in my original manuscript.

My appreciation to Laura Williams McCaffrey: Your wise words and deep understanding of speculative fiction were so helpful. Thank you for your encouragement and support.

To Diane Ferlatte: Your passion and gift for storytelling are an inspiration. Thank you for the generous gift of your time and expertise as I sought to develop the character of Miss Inniss and the storytelling culture of the book.

Thank you to my educator colleague Gail Lima for her marine science expertise and feedback on the latter chapters in the book. Thank you also to my student and advisee Catherine Anderson for her feedback on scuba diving equipment and the certification training required for a young diver.

First Five Pages Workshop: Thank you, Martina Boone, Erin Cashman, Lisa Gail Green, and fellow writers in the July 2016 cohort, for your helpful critiques and encouragement.

Thank you to the wonderful writers and teachers I have learned from as I work to improve my craft. To GrubStreet, LitReactor, Inked Voices, Writers.com, the Writers' Loft in Sherborn, and the Solstice MFA program at Pine Manor College, thank you!

To Kentucky Country Day School: Thank you for your years of encouragement and personal support. In particular, thank you for honoring me with the Alumni Association Exceptional Teaching Award in 2013, which I used to start my journey as a professional writer. Thank you also to my colleague Marjorie Seely, who planted a seed when she suggested, "You should write a book."

To my friends and colleagues at The Winsor School, thank you for welcoming me into the community. Much thanks to my students for writing along with me over the years and being my inspiration. With love, Ms. S.